Jen,

Buckle up ___ 'e
will continue fast r.
Furious

LET ME
SAY THIS, AGAIN

by
B. Swangin Webster

B. Swangin Webster

ISBN-13: 978-1-940758-04-6

Cover Design by Instinctivedesign

Published by:
Intrigue Publishing
11505 Cherry Tree Crossing Rd. #148
Cheltenham, MD 20623-9998

Printed in the United States of America
Printed on Recycled Paper

LET ME
SAY THIS, AGAIN

Dedication

I would like to dedicate this to all the future authors. Your dream of being an author, as long as **you** believe in it, will come true.

Chapter 1

Matthew woke up by himself. He found his pants and pulled them up his muscular legs and then set about the house to find her. He walked upstairs and found the unmade bed. He saw the bathroom door closed and walked up to it, hoping she was behind it. He knocked and not a sound so he pushed it open. Still no Cheryl. He proceeded down the hall into her study and still did not find her. He descended the stairs and walked into the kitchen where an empty cup sat in the sink but there was no coffee made only the tea ball on the counter. He looked at the table, where the plates had been and then opened the dishwasher. He smiled as she must have gotten up and ran it late last night. He walked back into the living room and sat on the couch. Maybe she had went to work already, he thought to himself as he stood and stretched.

He pulled his sweater on and as he headed out the front door he found the note. He read it over and over, then crumpled the paper in his hand and went to his car, letting the door slam behind him.

He got home and needed to figure out how he was going to find her. He sat at his desk and thought about the note. She said she needed time to think, time to sort things out. She always spoke about going to Florida whenever she felt stressed and he hoped his hunch was right.

He arrived at the airport hoping to find a seat on the first thing out of D.C. to Florida. "Good afternoon, I am hoping that you can help me," he said as he walked up to the counter, "I am trying to get a first class seat to Florida."

"Oh, sir, I'm sorry. All of our flights to Florida are totally booked. Matter of fact, we have some passengers on stand-by trying to get there. With this crazy weather we are having everybody wants to get out of town. You know a little snow and people want to head for the sun."

"Well, it's a matter of life and death. He smiled and leaned against the counter. "I would appreciate it."

"Let me check for you."

She started tapping keys and looking at the screen. "I'm sorry, sir, there is nothing. Even if there were, I would be obligated to get these other passengers on first, since they have been waiting for over two hours."

"Please, can you look again?"

Again she went back to tapping the keys. She spoke just above a whisper. "Well there is a flight that has a seat, in first class, but it is going to run you at least nine hundred and fifty-two dollars, and that's before all of the fees."

"I'll take it!" he handed her his black American Express card

"The flight is leaving from Gate 12 in twenty minutes. Do you have any bags that you need checked?"

"No."

She printed out the boarding pass and handed it to him.

"Thank you very much, Linda. You just made me the happiest man in the world. I will never forget this."

"No problem. Enjoy yourself, Mr. Perry," she said with a smile.

Matthew rushed down the concourse and was stopped in his tracks by the security line snaking all the way past the food court. He excused himself and he walked around people and then gave up and walked around the barriers. He walked up to the small podium and handed his license and his boarding pass to the security officer.

"Sir, you can't just walk up here, these people are in front of you."

"And my flight is leaving in ten minutes and I have to be on it."

"Sir, you have to wait your…"

"I'm sorry, I gave you the wrong ID." Matthew said as he pulled out his government issued CAC card. Now, I am assuming that I can proceed?"

"Sorry Mr. Perry. Yes, please go ahead."

Matthew placed his bag on the conveyor belt and walked through the scanner. Glancing at his watch, he saw they were boarding in less than five minutes. His stride was long and hurried but he got there just as he attendant was making final call for boarding. He handed her his ticket and made his way to the plane.

After taking his seat in first class, Matthew called the flower shop within the airport and had them make a special arrangement for Linda, just to show his appreciation. After taking his seat, he quickly took out his laptop, and logged into his AOL account. He shot off a quick note to his business partner and told him what was going on and asked him to call the Sheraton in Miami and book him a room. Matthew sat back, closed his eyes and thought just how lucky he had been.

Her flight landed late and she was too wired to go to sleep. She sat up all night thinking of Matthew and how she should have told him where she was going.

Her phone rang, breaking her trance. She answered it.

"Where the fuck are you?" came the irate voice from the other end

"None of your business."

"It's my fucking business when you up and leave Kayla with your parents and don't tell them where the fuck you are going."

3

"Kevin, look, whatever I do or don't do is none of your business."

"Don't get cute with me. I am not going to have you running off whenever the mood strikes you."

"What do you care, what kind of mood I'm in?"

"Bitch!"

She pressed the end button and set the phone down. It began to ring again. She looked at the caller id but didn't recognize the number. She started to let it ring but she needed to make sure that her daughter was ok.

"Hey sexy. Don't think you are going to get away from me that easily. I'll see you soon."

She didn't get to say anything because the caller hung up. It wasn't a voice she recognized. She went to the bathroom and decided to soak in some bubbles for a little while before starting her day.

Chapter 2

Matthew arrived in Florida to rain and wind. He mumbled as he slid his keycard into the door. He walked in and cranked the heat to 75 and felt sleep weighing down on him. Just as he pulled his shirt above his head, his cell rang.

"Hello?"

"Is this Matthew Perry?" the husky voice inquired.

"Who's asking?" Matthew asked while looking at the phone.

"Answer the question."

"I ain't answering anything until you tell me who this is." He said as he wrote down the number on the notepad by the bed.

"Well, I think I have my answer, so to answer yours–this is the past coming back."

He hung up and tried to get back to get some sleep. He couldn't because something about that voice felt familiar to him. He picked up the notepad and stared at the number.

"Hey mom, how is Kayla?"

"Mad," She wanted to go with you, can't say I blame her. She hardly gets to see you, now that you are working and now you just jump up and go to Florida. I guess now that you have a man, she hardly gets to see you anymore."

"What is that supposed to mean?" Cheryl asked.

"Don't act like you didn't know that Matthew called here looking for you, like he didn't know…"

"Mom, I am not here with Matthew. I don't know where he is. So let me guess, this is the reason why Kevin is being a plum fool because you told him that I was here with Matthew, huh?"

Silence.

"I can't believe you mom, all I asked you to do was to keep Kayla for me and asked you not to tell anyone where I was going. Now I have to be looking over my shoulder for his crazy ass."

"You watch your tone with me, Missy, that boy still loves you…"

"Really, you are going to say that to me? First of all, he has been cheating on me for over two years with Rebecca. Secondly, he would beat me almost on a daily basis and lastly, how about he almost killed me? So don't tell me about him still loving me, if he loves someone, it sure as hell aint me!"

"As I was saying, that boy loves you like no other, and for you to be traipsing around here like some tramp…"

"Goodbye, mother." Cheryl pressed end and threw the phone on the bed.

Matthew dressed quickly and ran down to the lobby and asked the front desk where the nearest flower shop was.

The sky was clearing and it might just be a good day after all, he thought to himself, as he found the flowers that he wanted. He whistled as he walked back in and walked to the front desk counter.

"Can you have these delivered to the room of Mrs. Cheryl Bookman."

The woman took the flowers and sat them to the side. He walked towards the chairs in the lobby and took a seat. Patience was not what he was known for but in the case he had to show some.

He saw the woman with the beige pants and hotel polo shirt take the flowers from behind the desk and head towards the elevators. As she stepped in and the doors began to close, he yelled for her to hold the elevator.

"Nice flowers." He commented to her.

"Yes, someone is going to love these." She said as she smelled the yellow roses.

The elevator stopped on the twelfth floor and the woman got off with Matthew behind her.

"Have a great day." He said to her as he continued past the door that the woman stopped in front of. He continued down the hall and rounded the corner. When he heard the elevator ding its arrival he walked back around the corner and straight to Cheryl's room.

He knocked and waited for her to answer and when she did, he grabbed her into his arms and kissed her before she could say a word.

"Well, hello to you too." she said.

"So are you going to invite me in?" he said.

She stepped aside and he walked in and stood next to the door.

"So I am assuming you sent these to me."

"Guilty." He said with a huge smile on his face.

"Thank you so much. You sure know how to make a woman feel special."

"Good because I wasn't sure if you were upset with me."

"I just felt like I needed to get away." She stood and got the brush from the dresser. She began brushing her hair.

He walked behind her, taking the brush from her and began to brush her hair. "No need to apologize. I'm just glad that I found you."

"How did you find me?"

"I am a very resourceful man when I need to be. Would you do the honor of accompanying me to dinner this evening?"

"Well since you went through all this trouble, sure." She said as she stood and kissed his cheek and walked him to the door.

"Good, I'll be back to pick you up around five. Oh, and make sure you don't change. I like seeing you in those jeans."

As he walked back to his room, his phone began to ring. He saw his daughter's picture flashing on the screen. .

"Hey baby girl. What's up? What! Put your mother on the phone."

She came on the line and immediately started yelling.

"Look, don't fucking ask me shit! Ask your daughter why she brought in two D's on her damn report card. Always calling me asking what I'm doing to this little brat!"

Matthew kept his voice calm because he knew this would become a shouting match without any effort on his part.

"I am not going to tell you again about calling her names. Put her back on the phone"

After a few seconds Tamia came to the phone.

"Tamia? What is your mom talking about... you got D's on your report card?"

"Mommy wouldn't let me go to the choir concert so I got marked a grade down for that and then she didn't bring my project to school. She knew it wouldn't fit on the bus."

"Put mommy back on the phone."

He could hear the yelling in the background.

"Look, I don't want to hear it. Get your ass in your room and stay there until I tell you to come out, and stop stomping your damn feet before I whoop your ass! What do you want?" Sherrie shouted into the phone

"I have told you about a million times about the way you talk to her. I am not going to tell your trifling ass anymore. Why didn't you take her project to school?"

8

"Look, don't ask me a thing. Why didn't you bring your ass over here and take it your damn self!"

"Look from now on, I will have one of the limos take her to school, that way she doesn't have to wait for your whoring ass to do something!"

"Fuck you!"

"I'm sure you have already done that to someone else today."

He disconnected the call as the curse words hung in the air like cheap perfume.

Chapter 3

Cheryl finished up her spa treatment just as her phone rang.

"Where in the hell have you been?" Dee screamed into the phone "I have been worried sick about you."

"For what, I'm fine. I'm in Florida, chilling."

"Look, Kevin has been calling here acting weird, saying stuff like he is going to get you because you left Kayla. Where is my god daughter?"

"Dee, are you serious? She is with my parents. You know how Kevin is, don't pay him no never mind."

"Look, just be careful. Remember that poor woman whose boyfriend went to her job and poured gas on her. I don't want that happening to you, you know he is a damn nut and I don't have anybody to bail me out if I whoop his ass!"

"Look, stop being so dramatic. I'm here in Florida and I am not dealing with him on that level anymore."

"Good for you but I hope you are getting your freak on in Freaky Florida."

"Get your mind out of the gutter. Matthew just arrived and we are going to have dinner.

"I bet you are," Dee said seductively.

"It ain't that kind of party.. Not doing that again until I'm sure I am ready to handle it."

"Whatever. Just don't wait too long, I'm sure there are other fish in the sea waiting for him to swim by. Talk to you later, girl."

She hung up just as she got in front of her hotel door. A smile crept on her face when she saw another dozen yellow roses sitting beside the first. Her phone rang again as soon as she was inside.

"Hello."

"Hello, sweetness," the male voice said.

"Who is this?"

"Someone who wants to get to know you as well as Matthew does." The phone went dead and her hands were shaking. She nearly jumped from her skin when there was a knock on the door

"Who…who is it?" she asked.

"It's me. Matthew." She quickly opened the door and fell into his arms "Man, maybe I need to surprise you more often."

She tried to calm herself but her heart was racing. He pulled back from her as he felt the small tremor coming from her

"Wait, what's wrong?" He said as he led her to the desk chair, "Is it Kevin?"

"I don't know. Someone just called my phone. Called me sweetness and said they want to know me like you know me."

"Look, calm down. It's probably just some kids."

"I don't know. I have heard that voice before. He has called the house. I thought it was some of Kayla's friends, but I guess…" She reached for her inhaler and took a hit from it like a crack addict on the pipe.

"Look, give me your cell. I'll try and find out who it is." Matthew took the phone and walked in the other room. He called his contact at the phone company.

"Yes, can you block any and all unknown or private numbers to this phone? Yeah, and thanks, I owe you one." Matthew said as he walked back over to Cheryl "Now, just calm yourself down, and I'll get you some water."

Chapter 4

Matthew took her sightseeing and to the beach where they lay around until they were hungry and then they each retired to their own rooms. Heading back into the real world would be hard but it was made much easier now that she was giving Matthew a chance to win her heart. Cheryl was comfortable with the way they had talked things through and she was beginning to see that she was deserving of a man like Matthew. They left Florida together after three days.

She was preparing for another date with Matthew when the phone rang,

"Ma, telephone!" Kayla yelled upstairs.

"Hello, sweetness," said the husky voice on the other end. "Going out tonight?"

"Who is this?"

The phone went dead.

"Kayla! Get up here! Who do you have calling here?" she said as her daughter stood in the doorway of the bathroom.

"Nobody, why you always accusing me?" Kayla said while smacking her lips together.

"Look, I've told you before, don't give out this number. I don't want every Tom, Dick and Jerome calling here."

"How do you know it wasn't for you?"

"Cause they hung up when I asked them who it was. Now if

your friends can't be civil, then they can't call here. Do you understand me?"

Kayla glared at her mother, "Well, dad…"

Cheryl cut her off, "You're not at your dad's house! So if that is what you were about to say, don't."

Kayla stormed out of the hallway and into her room. Just then the phone rang again.

"Don't touch it. I'll get it," Cheryl snatched up the receiver. "Look, I don't know who in the hell this is, but you better stop calling my house."

"Oh. I'm sorry. I was looking for the woman I was going to be meeting later tonight but if you have changed your mind all you had to do was say so," Matthew said.

"I'm sorry. Some of Kayla's friends are playing on this phone again. Ugh. I swear that girl will be…"

"Stop, no negative thoughts tonight. This night will be all about you. Now, is Kayla going to her girlfriend's house? You know I don't like her being there by herself."

"Yes, as a matter of fact, I have to drop her off before meeting you at the club."

"Don't be late. I have special plans for you, sweetness."

"What did you just call me?" I asked.

"Sweetness, why?"

"Did you call here about ten minutes ago?"

"No."

She shook the negative thoughts from her head. "Never mind me. I'll see you in thirty minutes." She hung up and started humming and then called Kayla to hurry up.

Kayla came bouncing downstairs with her sleeping bag and overnight bag.

"Do you have everything? You know I am not coming back here."

"I know. Dang," she said, with the smacking of the lips again.

14

"Look, Kayla, stop being such a smart ass. I don't have time for this. I am sick of your smart mouth. Just stop acting…"

"Like what…?"

"What has gotten into you lately?" Kayla said as she picked up her keys from the table in the foyer.

"Nothing, can we just go?"

After dropping Kayla off at Tamia's house, she headed off to meet Matthew at Club E. She walked in and found him standing near the bar.

"Malibu for her and rum and Coke for me, please," Matthew said as he put his arm around her. "You are looking very sexy tonight," he whispered into her neck as he kissed her cheek.

"And so are you" she answered.

Suddenly, everyone's attention was on the dance floor. An older man, maybe around the age of sixty, hit the dance floor by himself. He started to slow dance by himself. He had cream colored slacks with a cream colored shirt. He had on snake skin cowboy boots and had the sexiest salt/pepper hair. He danced to *One in a Million* by Bobby Womack. He raised his arms above his head and proceeded to turn his back to Cheryl's side of the club and slid his hands down his head and onto his shoulders. He slowly turned around and faced her and when he finished his perfect turn, he swayed down to the floor, all while rubbing his hands all over his body.

For some reason he locked eyes with Cheryl, and she couldn't look away. The women in the club were going wild, throwing money at him and one woman came onto the dance floor with him and starting putting money at his feet. The song ended with him in a deep bow. The crowd gave him a standing ovation.

Freak-um Dress Remix came on by Beyoncé.

"Care to dance on the floor instead of in your chair?" Matthew asked while pulling her up.

"If you can keep up," she said and did a hip roll that had him stumbling backwards.

He grabbed her hips and pulled her towards him and they moved like two ballroom dancers. The next song came on by Ja Rule, *Where Would I Be Without You,* she pressed herself against him and he against her. His manhood grew as she gyrated her hips against him and they fell back into a seductive dance.

The songs ended and they decided to head back to their table for one last drink before he asked for the tab. He whipped out his credit card and left a hundred on the table for the waitress. He pulled Cheryl into a kiss as they reached the sidewalk.

"I don't want this night to end," he said once they broke the kiss.

"Neither do I," she moaned back.

"Come back with me. I promise you, you will not be sorry."

Chapter 5

They drove for about twenty minutes and finally pulled off Route 210 onto the access road behind C&D carry out and she pulled her SUV behind his.

"I have to enter the code, but follow close behind me so the gate doesn't close," he said while leaning into her black Lexus RX300.

"Ok."

After driving about a mile he got out and trotted up to her car and opened the door. As he unlocked the door, she ran her hand down his back. They walked in and he disabled the alarm, and set his keys on the table on the left side of the door.

"Can you point me to the bathroom?"

"Sure, just down the hall to the right. Care for a night cap?" he said while untying his tie.

"Oh no, you aren't going to have me all liquored up."

"Right, I want you in your right mind when I have my way with you," he said with a wink.

She disappeared down the hall and when she came out she walked toward the music.

He had some nice jazz playing and he was in the kitchen.

"Thought you might like a little something, so I called ahead and had some fruit taken out for you," he said, while seductively eating a piece of strawberry.

"How nice of you," she said as she admired his kitchen. The

cabinets were dark mahogany and the floors were dark cherry hardwood. He had stainless steel appliances and black granite countertops. He had a latte station under one cabinet and a flat screen television inside of the refrigerator door.

He had apple cinnamon candles lit and had just poured himself a drink.

"Sure you won't join me?"

"Positive. I still have to drive home. I can't stay long." She said as she popped a couple of grapes in her mouth.

"Well, feel free to stay here, I do have extra rooms."

"That won't be necessary. I'll just eat your fruit and be on my way," she said with a smile.

"Well, there is something I would like to eat and it damn sure ain't this fruit," he said while walking up behind her. He wrapped his arms around her waist and nuzzled into her neck.

"O-ok, don't start anything you don't intend on finishing." She said

"Don't worry. I intend on finishing what I start." His hands went up her skirt and stopped when he reached her hips.

"I don't wear them...," she said while turning to face him.

His hands continued around to her round bottom and his huge hands cupped it just hard enough to elicit a moan from her. He continued kissing her neck, easing down to her breast.

His hands were now under her shirt, kneading her nipples like a baker kneading his dough. He started licking down her stomach and when he got to the waistband of her skirt, he unzipped and yanked it down in one motion. He dove between her legs like she was a pool. He licked her most sensitive flesh like an ice cream cone. Her hands reached for something, anything that she could hold onto. She closed her legs around his head.

"Oh, no you don't. I want to taste every inch of you," he moaned.

18

"I-I can't stand."

"No need," he said, while lifting one leg up onto his shoulder.

"Wa-wait, I'm going to fall."

"I got you."

She moaned louder.

"Yeah, baby. Give it to me," he moaned back.

"Oh, God!" She screamed while grasping his shirt. She was breathing like an African who had just won the marathon in the Olympics. He lowered her to the floor and kissed her hard.

She started to unbutton his shirt. He reached around and unfastened her bra and slid the shirt from her shoulders. Her hands ran down his back, causing him to shudder.

"Damn, you sure know how to touch a brotha," he whispered.

"I try." She moaned into his ear.

"But tonight is all about you," he said while holding her breasts.

He leaned down and began sucking them while she continued to rub his back.

"Damn I need more of you," he said while lifting her onto the center island. He pushed the fruit bowl to the side and pushed her legs wide open.

"Oh, my goodness, Matthew, what are you trying to do to me?" He gripped her hips harder and pulled her back to his mouth. His tongue worked harder and faster, then slower and soft.

"C'mon and give it to me Cheryl, let me taste you again."

Her legs began to shake, her breaths were quick and her heart was racing.

"Ummm, baby." He groaned and pushed his fingers deeper inside of her.

Her moans came out in a continuous undiscernible stream.

"You like that don't you?" he said as he stood directly in front of her

"Y-Yes."

"Oh, but I am not finished with you yet." Matthew took her hands and pulled her from the countertop. He lay down on the floor and said, "Sit down. I want you in control."

"I- I don't think."

"It's not about thinking. It's about doing. Now, come here," he said, while pulling her down onto his face. As soon as she was close enough, his tongue reached into her private space and began a whole new assault.

"I like to watch you," he whispered.

"And I like the way you watch me," she whispered back.

"Um-hmm. That's the way I like it," he moaned. "You are a very sexy woman, Cheryl."

"And you are a very hungry man, Matthew," she said as her senses heightened and she plunged into the erotic world yet again.

She was weak and sweaty. Matthew pulled her up and carried her to the shower.

"Let me bathe you…if you don't mind," he said while setting her down. He turned on the shower, angled the six shower heads and adjusted the water, he turned up the speakers so the jazz funneled through.

"I insist that you join me,"

He asked, "Shall I use apple and cinnamon or are you a flower type of girl?"

"Well, since we started the night off with fruits, let's stick with that, shall we?" she said

He angled the shower heads so that they hit her back, her breasts and her pubic area.

"Turn around for me," he said, He slid the sponge between her legs and let it rest there for a minute. Before moving on, he let his fingers slide inside of her.

"Mmmm," she moaned.

"I need to be inside of you," he whispered in her ear. His manhood slid between her legs. She rose to the balls of her feet to take him all in. His hands cupped her breasts and he kissed the back of her neck.

"Umm. Mmmm." He moaned as he pushed himself harder into her. "You feel so good, Cheryl."

"I'm going to cum," he moaned into her ear. She pushed her ass harder into him and he pushed himself harder up into her. His hands came up and squeezed her nipples hard.

He continued pushing himself into her harder and harder.

"Ah, Matthew!"

"Yeah, baby!"

"Matthew!"

His moans were strained as he grabbed her hair and pushed into her one last time. He kissed the back of her neck and ran his hands down her back.

He was motionless for a few seconds before speaking.

"Whew. I have never experienced that before," he said while lathering the sponge and continuing what he initially started.

"What?" She asked.

"You make me want you all the time. When I think I am done your body makes me want you more. You are amazing," he said while rubbing the sponge up and down her body

"Me amazing? You got it all wrong," she said while taking the sponge and motioning for him to turn around. "You were incredible. You have skills and are not afraid to use them for the good of woman-kind.

"So, you are an ass woman?" He said jokingly as she slid the sponge up and down his round bottom.

"Definitely. I like something I can hold on to, and yours is perfect."

"I'm glad you like," he said.

"As much as I would love to stand here and explore you

more, I really must be getting home."

"Are you sure you can't stay?" He asked while turning off the water.

"Positive. However, I might just have to come back."

"I'll keep the shower ready for you."

He stepped out and handed her a towel, "Take your time. I'll be waiting for you in the kitchen. "

Chapter 6

"Matthew?" She said while walking into the kitchen where he stood with just a pair of jeans on. "Did you? I mean- When you…"

"Cheryl? What's wrong?"

"I-I-. Did you…you know…?"

"Did I what?" he asked as he set the knife on the counter.

"You know…" she said while raising her eyebrows.

"I'm not sure what you are talking about."

She turned her head slightly, clearly embarrassed to say the words.

"If you mean, did I cum? Well yes I did." He said with a smile.

Her face frowned and she rolled her eyes.

"What is that face about?"

"We didn't think. This could be trouble." She said

"Cheryl. It's ok. I'm safe. I trust you. I have only slept with four women my entire forty-five years, two being my girlfriends in college and then my wife for ten years and only one other person, and have always used a condom, except with my wife. It happened so fast. I'm sorry," he said while walking towards her.

"Sorry? That's all you can say. Sorry. What if I turn up pregnant? I'm too damn old for kids. Just because you say you're safe, doesn't mean that you are. Damnit I am so stupid!" She

23

grabbed her shoes and headed for the door.

"C'mon Cheryl. Wait. We had sex before…"

"Yes and we always used a condom…"

"Ok, we slipped up. It won't happen again…don't leave like this," he said while walking behind her.

He grabbed her arm and she gasped, flinched and yelled, "I'm sorry."

"What's the matter?" He was stunned at her over-reaction. Her eyes were batting fast and she began to stutter

"O…Ok…I'm sorry. I'm sorry."

"What the hell? Cheryl are you ok?"

"Yes, I'm sorry. I shouldn't have said anything…"

"Wait, what is going on with you?" he asked as he noticed her eyes darting around the room and she began breathing heavily.

"Nothing. I have to go." She said as she walked quickly to the door.

He reached for her and she let out another gasp. "What is wrong?"

"Nothing."

"It's something and you are not leaving her until you tell me." he said as he put his hand on the door.

She held her head down and held her hands. "Kevin–he used to…"

"Crap, I'm sorry. I'm sorry. I didn't mean to yell at you. I was just trying to stop you before…I'm sorry. I didn't mean to scare you." he said as he tried to hug her.

"I'm sorry. I have to go," she said as she stood just out of his reach. She turned quickly and bolted out of the door.

"Cheryl! Wait!" He ran out with no shoes on and came up to the car as she was opening up the door. "Cheryl," he said breathlessly. "Don't leave like this, please."

"I have to go. I'll call you."

"Promise me that you will as soon as you get home."

"Ok," she said as she started the engine.

"No, promise," he said

"I promise,"

She got home and dialed Dee. She didn't answer so she hung up but her phone rang immediately. She pulled her nightgown over her head and picked up the phone.

"Dee?" she said

"No, this is Matthew, and I thought you promised to call me when you got home."

"I just walked in the door."

"Look, we need to talk about what happened. I didn't mean not to use a condom. It was just…"

"Just what, Matthew? You know I am still in a custody battle with Kevin and he will use any and everything to convince the judge that I am an unfit mother."

"What does making love to me have to do with you being an unfit mother?"

"What if I get pregnant? He will say I am sleeping with god only knows how many men and he will take her away from me. You don't understand how hateful he is." She broke down into tears.

"Cheryl, I am sorry. Please don't be upset. "

"Whatever." She cut him off.

"No, not whatever. You are a very sexy, desirable woman and I have wanted to be with you since you let me take you to dinner that night. God knows, it took all I had not to make love to you in the limo. Then when you let me make love to you, I knew I was in heaven. Like I said, I have had only four partners, so this is not something I take lightly. I have gotten myself tested, every five years just for GP. So if you think I sleep with any and all women, you are mistaken." She heard the doorbell ringing.

"Look, I have to go. Someone is at the door," she said while walking down the steps.

"Don't let anyone in. It's late, and you never know who that could be."

"I will call you later," she said as she walked downstairs.

"No need," he said and hung up.

She opened the door, "Wh...What are you doing here?"

"I couldn't let this night end like this," he said while walking past her into the living room. "Plus, you didn't finish your fruit." He held up the bowl.

She stepped aside as he walked in and sat on the leather sofa in her living room. She retrieved small plates from the kitchen and joined him on the sofa. She pulled a strawberry from the bowl as he popped a few grapes into his mouth. The discussion turned to his feelings for her.

"Cheryl tonight was very special to me and I don't know any other way to make you understand that I wouldn't do anything to hurt you."

"Matthew, I know but I'm scared. I'm scared to let you in. I have only allowed one person to enter into this space." She pointed to the middle of her chest. "And we both know how that has turned out."

"I am not him. I will never be him. I couldn't hurt the one that I love. I know it will take time but all I am asking you, is to allow that time to happen. Don't shut me out, ok?"

She moved closer to him and laid her head onto his chest. "I will try." She whispered.

"That's all I ask."

"But until the divorce, I would much rather we use some form of protection."

He gave a hearty chuckle.

"What are you laughing at?"

"Because at least I know that you want some of this again."

"Oh, I'm not stupid." She laughed as he leaned forward and

kissed her. "Besides, you have the freshest fruit."

The continued to talk until she yawned a second time.

"That yawn tells me that you need some rest. So I will leave and let you get some rest." He stood and walked to her door. He turned and pulled her close to him.

"I love you Cheryl Bookman."

"I love you Matthew Perry."

They shared a passionate kiss until he broke the embrace. He ran his hand down the side of her face and smiled.

No other words were spoken after that, he simply pulled the door open and walked out.

He drove home thinking about how lucky he was to find a woman like her. After his failed marriage he didn't know if he would ever feel the way about a woman, the way he had felt before.

Matthew decided to take Terrence up on his offer three years after he got married. His wife wasn't happy when she found out that he was quitting his six figure job to go into business with a man whose business was failing.

"What in the hell do you mean you are going into the limo business? Have you forgotten that you have a baby?"

"No, I haven't. I'm thinking about the baby. You complain all the damn time that I am never home with you and Tamia, so this way, I figure I can spend more time with you and her."

"What in the hell are you going to do about the fucking bills around here?"

"Don't worry about it. I was able to save some money and it should take care of the house payment for at least a year, and the other bills will be covered. We will have to cut back on a few things for a while, but that shouldn't be a big deal."

"Like what?" she screamed and she threw her cup in the sink.

"Well for one, you can't go and get your hair done every

week, maybe more like once a month. Spa treatments are definitely out, as well as the weekly pedicures and manicures."

She began pacing back and forth like a caged animal.

"Are you crazy? I am not going to stop taking care of me just because you want to do something this stupid. Just pick up the phone and tell your firm that you had a change of heart and go back to them."

"See, this is what I mean. You aren't even trying to consider…"

"You damn right. I am not giving up what I have just so you can live out your dream."

"What are you giving up, Sherrie? I pay for you to get all that shit done. So if it wasn't for me, you wouldn't be doing it!"

"Whatever, nigga. You knew when we got married that I didn't want to work and I hope that you don't think I am going to start."

"God forbid that I ask you to pick up the slack, but to answer your question, I don't expect you to work, what I *do* expect, is for you to stop taking Tamia to daycare. If you want money stop the daycare and stay your ass home with her. If not, then find the damn money yourself!"

Matthew stormed out of the kitchen and went outside. He had to get away from her before he did something he didn't want to do, namely, hit her in the mouth. He made a promise to his mother that he would always treat women with respect. He saw his neighbor Brian. Brian was the first person to welcome them to the neighborhood years ago. They used to play spades almost every weekend until Sherrie got jealous, so that ended, but they were still cool.

"What's up dude?"

"Nothing just had to get out of the house for a bit." Matthew said walking up his driveway.

"Want to go out for a drink?"

"Sure, just let me tell Sherrie that I'll be back in a bit." He walked in on his wife on the phone with one of her friends.

"Look, I'm going out. Be back in a little while."

"Don't be so fucking rude. Don't you see me on the damn phone? Girl, I'll call you back." She hung up and turned to him. "How long do you plan on being gone? I told you earlier that I was going out with my girlfriends tonight, and I didn't get a babysitter."

"Well, get one. I don't know how long I'm going to be out. Brian and I are going to have some drinks."

Just then, Brian knocked on the door. Sherrie looked at him, rolled her eyes and snatched the cordless phone from the base.

"Are you going to leave some money here for the babysitter?"

Matthew reached into his pocket and pulled out a fifty, turned and walked out the door.

"Trouble?" Brian asked when he got to his car.

Matthew slid into the leather seat of Brian's BMW. "I just told her I resigned from my job to go into business, and let's just say she wasn't pleased."

"Well, congrats. There is nothing like it. I've been in the gardening business for a while and wouldn't trade it for the world. If I don't feel like going to work, I call my workers, tell them their assignments and then lay my white ass back down. What's your business?"

"I'm going to be working with limos."

"Man that is a great business. Prom, birthdays, weddings, girl's night out, anniversaries. Man, there is business out there waiting to be had. There is never a down time."

"Yeah, it doesn't hurt that the guy that I'm going to be partnering with has had the business for over fifteen years, so there is a client base already."

They arrived at the sports bar and grabbed a seat at the bar.

They enjoyed a few drinks and decided to get something to eat. As the waitress brought their food, they heard a loud group of women.

"Man, this place gets some hotties up in here," he said while looking around.

"I bet you try to holla at all of them, don't you?"

"I do what I can," he said while laughing. Suddenly a familiar face walked by.

"So, is this where you normally hang out?" Matthew asked when his wife walked up to the bar.

"No, the girls and I are on our way to the club. We just stopped in here to get some drinks before we go. Don't wait up," Sherrie said while walking away.

Matthew decided to call it a night and left Brian at the bar. He got home and told the babysitter she could leave, checked on his baby girl and then turned in.

He had trouble settling down for sleep but his mind stayed on his business. He was two months into the business and he had his hands full. Bringing a fledging business up to date was hard work but he enjoyed the challenge. His wife began to go out more and more since he was home and could make his own hours. He began noticing small things but didn't tell her about them because in the end, he would need to catch her at her own game.

The next day he came home from work and was hit by the argument as he walked in the door.

"You are always working!" she shouted.

"Because you are always spending money." He said as he shed his jacket.

"Whatever," she said, smacking her mouth.

"Not whatever, if you expect to keep up with your little

friends in the latest fashions, then stop complaining."

He took his daughter from his wife and started kissing her cheeks. "Look, did my mom call today?"

"I don't know. Maybe."

"And what is that supposed to mean?"

"It means, when doesn't she call? Damn, you would think..."

"Don't even start that shit again. I told you, if my mom calls me, just tell me."

"Damn, it's not like you are married to her. Why you have to talk to her everyday anyway? It's not like..."

He cut her off, "Don't you ever, as long as you are living here, question me about my mother, do you understand me?"

She mumbled under her breath and walked into the kitchen. He walked behind her and yanked her around to him.

"Get your damn hands off of me,"

He released her and she fell against the wall. He went into the bedroom to call his mom. He didn't like the fact that she had a new man in her life. His mom was his life and she deserved to be happy, just not with the guy she was currently seeing. He talked to his mom for almost an hour. When he walked out Sherrie was hanging up the phone.

"You better make sure that you have a sitter and you better be home before the sun comes up." he said as he walked past her.

She got up and walked into the kitchen. "I'll be in, when I get in. You ain't my father."

He walked in behind her, "I am not going to keep putting up with this shit from you."

"Whatever. I don't ever get to go anywhere, and the minute I do, you act like this."

"Are you serious? You have been going out every night for the past couple of months, and I am getting tired of it."

"Well, get used to it. I'm not stopping just because you said so."

31

Chapter 7

The argument with Sherrie lasted half the night and the other half was spent trying to get Shania to sleep.

Matthew woke up and felt as if something wasn't right. He couldn't put his finger on it but he just knew today wasn't going to be a good day.

He took a shower and cut himself while shaving, and while drinking coffee he wasted it on his green pinstriped shirt. While going to change, he fell going *up* the stairs. Now running late, he ran out of the house and promptly dropped his car remote in the small puddle of water that had formed at the front of the car. After shaking the remote off, he slid behind the wheel of his Mercedes and noticed the amber glow of the gas pump. "Shit, I knew she wasn't going to put gas in it," he said to no one in particular. He made it to the gas station but couldn't find his gas card, so he had to use the only money he had in his pocket. After filling up, he headed into the office and walked in while Karen was on a personal call.

"Chile, I told that nigga to get straight up out of my apartment. Please. He begged me so much, I ended up letting his ass stay the night, but woke him up bright and early and told him he had to roll."

Karen started laughing and finally noticed him standing there. "Oh, good morning, Mr. Perry." She said with her face flushed.

"Morning," he said with attitude. "I'll need to see you in my office."

He continued into his office, threw his briefcase on the chair and walked to the area that housed his mini bar and coffee pot. He poured himself a cup of coffee just as the phone rang. The voice on the other end immediately irritated him.

"...when I get there!" He slammed the phone down and rubbed his temple as the headache got worse.

Karen walked in the door and noticed him pressing his fingers on both sides of his head. She walked over to the wet bar, got a glass of water and pulled the Tylenol from the overhead cabinet.

"Here you go," she said as she handed him the glass and Tylenol.

"Thanks. You do know that I should fire you, right? I have told you over and over not to take personal calls at your desk and that your language is not appropriate while you are on the phone. However, its things like this that reminds me that you are a really good asset to the company, so instead I will do this. Starting tomorrow you will have a week off, without pay."

Her face dropped but she said nothing. After it was clear that he had said all he was going to say, she walked out. As the door closed, his phone rang again.

"What!" He yelled into the phone.

"And good morning to you too. Having a bad day?" Terry asked. He was the other half of M & T Limo Service.

"It can't get any worse," Matthew replied.

"Things will get better. Don't forget we have that meeting with the head of transportation of Alpine Hotel and Spa."

"I haven't forgotten."

"See you at two," he said before he hung up.

Matthew began to wonder if he was being too hard on his

wife. He decided to surprise her and go home for lunch, maybe take her and Tamia out to eat. He answered a few calls and checked most of his emails before eleven. He told Karen that he would be out of the office for a couple of hours and he left, pointed towards home. He decided to stop for flowers to make up for his bad mood this morning. He pulled into his driveway at 12:03. He didn't know why that time seemed important to him but for some reason his gut was telling him he should have stayed at work a little longer.

"Whatever, he aint going to find out unless you get a conscience all of a sudden."

"Well, that's my man, and this shit aint right." The male voice said.

"Look you are free man, I aint holding you hostage, but trust me when I tell you, if it aint you, then it will be someone else. Now come here and let me show you why you will never stop coming over."

Matthew walked around the corner and saw the hands on his wife's hips. The same hips that he had held last week when she wanted to 'feel close to him.'' The low moan she emitted was barely audible but he knew that sound all too well. He was frozen to the floor, unable to move, unable to speak.

"Brian, let me show you what I do best."

Matthew was hoping that those hands weren't the same hands that he had helped cook burgers on the grill two weeks ago. He was hoping that those hands weren't the same hands that helped him change the tire on his car last week. He was also hoping that those hands weren't the same ones that had played ball with him last night. But he knew that those hands could only belong to one person. Matthew took a step and the floor moaned as if it was relieved that he had finally moved.

"Did you hear that?" Brian asked.

"Hear what? I didn't hear anything. Besides, I'm a little too busy to be listening to anything." Brian pressed his hands into her hair.

Matthew moved through the rest of the week barely speaking to Sherrie. He wasn't ready to let her in on his secret. He was glad that Brian hadn't invited him to his house and that he didn't see him coming and going. He knew it could have gotten really ugly and he didn't want to be the angry black person of the neighborhood. He was in a meeting when his cellphone vibrated. He couldn't take the call because he knew this might be seen as disrespect, especially since it was his personal phone that was ringing. Immediately after the meeting he pulled out his phone and punched in his voice mail code and heard something that would change his life forever.

By the time Matthew rushed from of the office and to her apartment, the place was crawling with police and ambulances. Of course, all the people in the complex were out there with their opinions.

"It's a damn shame, what he did to her." Said the man with the missing tooth.

"I knew he would hurt her one day, but she didn't want to listen to me."

"I feel so bad for her." The woman with the child pulling at her skirt said.

"Well, y'all should be ashamed. Y'all heard him in there beating that woman, and didn't do anything to help her." said the woman with the scarf around her head.

"Hey, I aint getting involved." the toothless man said.

"And its people just like you who let this woman get hurt."

"She knew how he was, aint nuttin' I would have told her that she didn't know."

Matthew was finally able to ask someone who was hurt and when he found out he pushed his way through the crowd. He followed the ambulance to the hospital and stayed with her night and day. She lay in a coma, with her eyes swollen shut, she had a cut on her head that would require twenty-two stitches, and had a broken arm, pelvis and fractured jaw. Work didn't matter to him at this point all that mattered was that he wasn't there when she needed him the most. What mattered was that he wasn't able to protect the woman that meant more to him than his daughter. He felt her stir and leaned into her.

"I love you, sweet pea."

"I love you too," he said as a tear slipped down his cheek.

Those were the last words she heard from him as she died three days later. He decided when he left the hospital that nothing would keep him from finding the man that did this to his mother. He made arrangements for her funeral and made the motions of going through it. Nothing mattered except for revenge. Finding him was a challenge but not one that he didn't win. He saw him walk from the bar and fell into step behind him. He saw his chance when he ducked into an alley to relieve himself.

The first blow sent him to his knees, and the succession of blows continued until he was unconscious. The sirens interrupted what would have been the night this man died. Matthew stayed hidden until the police were gone and the ambulance took their newest patient to the local hospital. Matthew drove an extra 30 miles to the hospital to get his hand looked at and found out that he fractured it and broke two fingers, most likely when his hand connected with the concrete instead of the side of his victims head. He needed to call his wife to pick him up, which didn't go well since she now had to cancel her plans for a night out. He went into the guest bedroom and poured himself a stiff shot and stretched out across the bed.

He woke up with a massive headache, a queasy stomach and an empty bottle of Grand Marnier. He walked downstairs ready for a fight with his soon to be ex-wife.

"What do you mean you want a divorce?" Sherrie said while stirring the pot of Cream of Wheat on the stove.

He got his cup out of the cabinet and poured himself a cup of coffee. He dumped the sugar from the container into the cup and then opened the refrigerator to get the half and half.

"How about you have been fucking our neighbor for the past few months?" he said calmly. "You and Brian think you slick. He's lucky I didn't put a fucking bullet in his head. All I know is, today, I will be leaving this house, file for divorce and you will get what you deserve."

"So you think you are going to leave me and not give me anything. You better think again." She said as she threw the spoon in the pot and walked over to where he was standing.

"Get away from me. Lord knows how many men you have been screwing since we have been married. For all I know my baby girl might not be mine

"How dare you."

"How dare I? So tell me, have you ever thought about whether I was her father, or not."

The silence in the kitchen was louder than the phone ringing.

"Better answer that, it could be your new nigga wondering why I haven't left yet. Let him know I will be leaving soon."

"Whatever." She said as she walked out of the kitchen behind him. She reached for his shirt and he spun around quickly.

"Look, Sherrie, I don't know who you think you are, but it would be in your best interest not to push me."

"Or what?"

He walked away because he was determined to keep the promise he made to his mother.

Two years to the day, the divorce was final and she got the house and shared custody of Tamia. She didn't get anything of what she wanted because she was good, but his lawyer was better.

That was the night his friends got together and decided to take him out, and that is where he had first seen Cheryl. Yes, his life changed that night.

Some men just don't realize how good they have it, but he wasn't one of them.

He didn't realize he was daydreaming until his phone rang on his lap.

"Speak to me." Matthew said into the phone.

"Is that how you answer your phone," the husky voice on the other end said.

"Who is this?" he asked as he pulled the phone away from his ear and looked at the screen. The words "number unavailable" stared back at him.

"Your worst nightmare." A slight pause filled the air until he spoke again. "That new lady friend of yours looks might tasty."

"I am not asking again, who is this?"

The voice chuckled and the phone went dead. He immediately dialed his ex-wife. As soon as he heard her pick-up he started yelling.

"Who in the fuck you got calling my phone?"

"What in the hell are you talking about?"

"Look, Sherrie, you better not have some rough neck nigga around my daughter."

"You don't give orders here." She said before hanging up.

He screamed and then started hurling obscenities to the walls within his bedroom. He ran down into the basement and started punching the workout bag. He worked out for two hours and when he felt he had let out enough stress, he went upstairs and started the shower but before stepping in, he called her.

"Hey sexy. Did I wake you? Sorry, just wanted to make sure you are ok."

"I am. Now why are you really calling?" Cheryl asked with a hint of attitude.

"Ok, ok, good lord, you are cranky when you wake up."

"Yes, especially when I don't get anything for it," she said seductively.

"So I see we are wide awake now."

"When I hear that voice of yours, it wakes me up. Now what do you want?"

"Nothing really, just to tell you that I love you."

"What did you just say?" Cheryl asked.

"I love you. I have loved you for almost as long as I have known you."

"Oh, my goodness." she sat up and folded her leg underneath herself. She ran her hand through her unruly hair and tried to stop from smiling. "Well, I love you too."

"Really?"

"You make me smile, and you make me feel safe and secure. You are a wonderful dad, friend and being the most incredible lover I have known doesn't hurt either. You make me feel like a woman, deserving of something better. You treat me better than I treat myself." she paused. "So let me ask you, why do you love me?"

He spoke slowly, "You are the beat that keeps me living. You are the breath that keeps me breathing, you are the light that keeps shining and it doesn't hurt that you are the most sensual person I have ever known. The way your eyes glaze over when I make love to you is incredible. The way you hold me, the way you kiss me, damn, it's nothing like I've ever experienced. Your kiss is like a dive into your soul, you give of yourself completely."

"You are going to make me drive over there," she said.

"C'mon,"

"Nope, I think you have done enough for one evening. Good night, Mr. Perry."

"Good night, Ms. Bookman. I love you."

"I love you, too."

She disconnected her phone and smiled. Her phone rang just as she got back to her bedroom. She answered it without looking at the screen.

"Look, honey, I'm tired and have to get some sleep."

"Who in the hell do you think this is?' Kevin asked.

"Why are you calling here, it's after midnight."

"Where is Kayla?"

"In bed I hope. She is at her friend Tamia's house."

"Well, you guessed wrong. The police just called here and they picked her up for violating the curfew laws in DC."

"So you are just calling me?"

"I tried, but your ass was out gallivanting all around town with that nigga."

"Whatever. Is she with you?"

"No, I'm on my way to get her. She is at the 8th precinct on 8th and Calvary Street Northwest.

Chapter 8

Cheryl arrived at the precinct in just under thirty minutes and found Kevin and Kayla sitting at the desk of Officer Price. Kevin was looking like he could slap the taste from Kayla's mouth, and Kayla was sitting with her arms folded. Kevin's face was tight, his jaw twitching and his hands were balled into tight fists. His breath came fast and furious as the beads of sweat formed between his brows.

"Well Kayla, since this is the first time you have done this, I suggest you listen to your dad and not do this again," the officer said.

"Oh, I can guarantee you that you will not see her again," Kevin said through clenched teeth.

Cheryl extended her hand to the officer.

"Sit down," Kevin said nastily. "This is her mother. She lives with her," he said as if saying it left a bad taste in his mouth.

"Like I was telling her father, Kayla was caught down in Georgetown after eleven, which is an hour after the curfew for D.C. Now, since this is her first offense, this is merely a warning. However, her name will now be in our data base and if she is caught out here again, she will be detained until at least morning. Then you and her dad will have to come to juvenile court."

Kayla stood as her mother approached the desk. The black leggings were hugging her curves like a snake wrapped around its prey. The makeup around her eyes made them appear to be cat like and the dark lipstick masked the immature lips of a fifteen year old.

"Where in the hell did you get those clothes?" Cheryl asked.

"You should have been asking her that, before your dumb ass dropped her off."

"You come on here, young lady, we will discuss this at home," she said as she grabbed Kayla by the arm. Kayla pulled away from her. Kevin shot Cheryl a look as Kayla brushed by them on her way out of the door.

"Thank you officer, you will not be seeing her again, I assure you of that." Cheryl said as she turned toward the officer.

As they neared Cheryl's SUV, Kevin grabbed her by the arm.

"What are you doing?" she asked him as she pulled her arm away from him.

"You are nothing but a tramp. Can you not flirt with every man that smiles at you? If you cared more about your daughter than screwing some nigga, then you would know what she was doing out here until almost midnight."

"I dropped her off at her girlfriend's house this evening. She didn't have those clothes on and…"

"I should slap the shit out of you right here!" Kevin yelled while walking over to Kayla.

"Look, you need to lower your voice. Yelling like a damn mad man ain't settling anything."

"Who the fuck do you think you are talking to?" He grabbed Cheryl's arm again just as a police officer passed.

"Sir, is there a problem?" he said as he stopped in front of them.

"Uh, no officer. No problem, just teenager issues," Kevin said.

"Mom, I'm sorry. We just wanted to see a movie and Tamia's friend Raelynn said we would be home before midnight. We got out at ten and we were at the subway station, but then a big crowd came on the platform and I didn't get on the train. I didn't have any way to get home, so I was trying to find a payphone to call her to come back and get me, I'm sorry. I didn't have any clothes that looked nice enough to go to the movies so I borrowed some of hers."

"This doesn't not excuse the fact that you were in a place that I didn't know about."

"The only place showing the movie was in Georgetown, I didn't think you would mind.

"Well, you should have asked me. Well, you certainly learned something tonight, didn't you? You gotta be quick when it comes to getting on the train."

As they pulled in front of the townhouse, Kayla hopped out and went into the house

"Where the fuck is she going?" Kevin asked.

"I told her to go to her room." Cheryl said while walking behind him into the house.

"You get your little ass down here right now!" He yelled up the stairs.

"Lower your damn voice," Cheryl whispered.

"Who in the fuck do you think you are? You got that girl out here at all hours of the night and then I have to be called to pick up her ass from the police station and you tell me to lower my damn voice. Bitch, I should take your fucking head off!" He had raised his hand just as Kayla came back down the stairs. He grabbed her before she was at the bottom.

"Get off of me!" Kayla said while yanking her arm away from her father.

"Take your hands off of her!" Cheryl said while grabbing for his shirt.

"Maybe if you spanked her ass, she wouldn't be out here doing god knows what. But I'll teach her tonight."

He yanked her into the bedroom and slammed the door shut and locked it. Cheryl banged on the door until her hand hurt. Suddenly the door flung open. He pushed past her and stomped down the stairs. Cheryl looked over at her daughter who was sitting on the bed, holding her face.

"Are you ok?" she asked as she sat down on the bed and rubbed her daughters back. Her daughter nodded and Cheryl rose and walked downstairs.

"Don't you ever put your hands on her again!"

"Get out of my face!" He said while drinking a glass of water.

"This is my house!" She yelled.

He threw the glass against the wall, and grabbed Cheryl by the shirt and slapped her. He then pushed her against the wall and had his fist balled up.

"You better take better care of her, or so help me, you will regret it." He slammed the door open and walked out.

Cheryl was on her knees picking up the broken pieces of glass.

"Mom, I will help you."

"I got it." Cheryl said.

"Mom..."

"I said I got it!"

Kayla stood and watched her mother on her knees picking up the glass and pulled her phone from her pocket. She kneeled down, took the cloth from her, and got more ice. She handed it back to her mother as her mother stood and faced her. Kayla slowly wrapped her arms around her mother and stood silent for ten minutes before breaking the embrace and heading out of the kitchen.

About an hour later, the doorbell rang.

"Who is it?"

"Open the door, Cheryl."

She pulled the door open when she heard Matthew's voice.

"Are you ok? Kayla called me. Let me look at your face. He hit you!"

"Matthew, calm down. I'm fine."

Matthew walked to the bottom of the stairs, "Kayla! Come down here."

"Matthew, I'm fine. Calm down."

"Look, the two of you are staying with me tonight."

"That is not necessary. Kayla, go back upstairs and get ready for bed." Kayla walked back upstairs and Cheryl heard her daughter's door close.

Matthew was staring at her when she turned back around.

"Cheryl, don't let that motha…."

"Shh, lower your voice." she said as she walked towards the kitchen.

"I'm sorry. It's just that I can't believe that motha-I mean I can't believe that nigga had the nerve to put his damn hands on you. I should find him and beat the shit out of him. He is not going to be putting his hands on the woman I love. Not going to happen, Cheryl. Look, you can't let him get away with this. You can't. If he did it tonight, he will do it again."

"Matthew come and sit down. Listen. It won't happen again, and if it does I will call the police, myself. Now, Kayla got herself into some trouble tonight by being downtown after curfew, he was upset and that is all."

"That doesn't give him the right to put his hands on you. He ain't even your husband anymore and he is still pulling rank!"

"Stop it. I said I would handle it. Now let it go. Please."

Kayla came bouncing into the kitchen full of energy.

"Mom, I left my stuff at Raelynn's house. Can you take me to get it?"

Matthew spoke up. "I'll take you, your mom is tired, let her rest for a little while.

"Can I, mom?"

"If Matthew doesn't mind, sure."

Kayla disappeared and Matthew walked in the kitchen. He pulled the cabinets opened and closed and he came back in with coffee for both of them.

"We have to talk about what he did last night. I will not put up with him man-handling you. Now if you need me to set you up with a bodyguard."

"Are you kidding me? He only slapped me."

Matthew's jaw clenched.

"Are you kidding me?"

"We were both stressed last night and he probably..."

Matthew held his hand up as he stood. "Don't you dare excuse his behavior to me."

"Let's not get into this again." Cheryl stood and steadied herself against the sofa.

"What's the matter?"

"Nothing," she said.

"Are you sure? You look a little flushed." He said as he placed his hand on her arm.

Cheryl went into the kitchen and poured out her coffee, suddenly feeling sick to her stomach. After they left, she stretched out on the couch and fell asleep.

The phone rang and she opened her eyes to see that she had been asleep for almost an hour.

"Hello."

"Let me talk to Kayla." Kevin said into the phone.

"She's not here."

"You let her go..."

"Matthew took her to pick up her things and to get her something to eat."

"I told you I didn't want him around her. Bring her over here

46

when she gets back."

"For what?"

"You heard what the hell I said."

Kayla came running up the stairs.

"Mom, Matthew took me and Raelyn to IHOP for breakfast. Mom you will never guess who's his daughter...Tamia...Tamia is his daughter. Can you believe that?"

"Seriously? Why haven't I ever seen you before when I dropped of Kayla for cheerleading practice?" She said to Matthew as they walked into her room. Not that she had actually seen Tamia's mom either. She dropped her off a couple of times after cheerleading practice, but never bothered to talk to her. She was like a lot of parents that used cheerleading practice as a babysitter. Cheryl couldn't recall seeing either of them in the two years that Kayla had been cheering.

"Small world, isn't it?"

"Mom, Matthew said he would take us downtown later."

"Kayla. Now after that stunt you pulled last night, don't press your luck. Besides, your dad called and wants you to come over there, so go get ready."

"I don't want to."

"Well, either I take you or he comes and gets you."

She stomped upstairs and slammed her door. Matthew came up and sat down on the couch beside her.

"Hey."

"Hey, yourself." She said as she snuggled up to him and put her arm across his chest.

"What's wrong?'' she asked him.

He got up and walked into the bathroom and came out with a washcloth and mirror. He handed them both to her.

She put the mirror in front of her and as the bruised face looked back at her, Matthew spoke.

47

"See…he is still leaving his mark on you."

"Matthew, look, I'm sorry. What do you want me to say?"

"Nothing, I want you to call the police."

"No."

"Then there is nothing you can say to me." He said as he walked out of the living room.

"Wait. Don't leave. I have to drop off Kayla at his house. Will you go with me?" she said as she stood and went to him.

After about an hour, Kayla was ready to go and Cheryl had covered up the bruise the best way she knew how. They drove in silence and Matthew pulled behind Kevin's BMW in the driveway. Kayla got out first and Cheryl climbed out slowly, like a dead man walking his last few steps.

"Should I go in with you?" Matthew asked.

"No, I should be fine." She said as she shut the car door.

Kayla walked in after he answered the door. She went straight up the stairs.

"Can we talk for a minute?" Cheryl said while walking further into the foyer.

"Talk," he said while walking towards his office.

"Can we talk in the living room?" He continued into his office but she refused to follow him.

"Look, we can talk in here. Now what in the hell do you want?"

"Kevin, look. I can't go in there. So I would appreciate…"

"This is my fucking house. If you can't talk in here, leave."

As she walked closer to the door, her hands began sweating and she rubbed them down the legs of her pants. She swallowed hard and then pulled her inhaler from her purse.

"Still using that thing, I see." He said as he blew out a harsh breath.

"Whatever, "I- I--"

"Will you spit it out? I don't have all fucking day. What is your problem?"

"You actually are going to ask me that, knowing what you did to me in here?"

"What did I do to you in here?"

"What! Are you serious? You raped me in here," she whispered, looking around as if someone would hear her.

"That's what you say."

"No, it's what happened. You and I both know it."

He rose from his desk and walked over to her.

She held her hands up, "Look, Kevin, I just want to talk."

"You say some shit like that to me and now you want to talk. What do you have to talk about?" he said as he backed her up to the door.

"Last night...you hit me, and you know I could have..."

He put his hand up to the door, causing her to flinch.

"You could have what...what could you have done, Cheryl? If you knew what in the hell Kayla was doing, I would not have been called to pick her up from the police station. So you tell me what you should have been doing?"

"I should have called the police. You are not my husband anymore and you should not put your hands on me. You left a huge bruise on the side of my face: one that I had to cover up before bringing her here today."

"So...that's my problem?" He said while walking back towards his desk.

"You damn right it is," she yelled. "You can't keep hitting me. We have been divorced for over two years. In all of the 20 years we were married, I never told anyone what happened while we were married. There is nothing to stop me from..."

"From what?" He yelled while slamming his hand onto the desk. "Don't you ever think about threatening me!" He said while jumping up from his desk and moving towards her.

"I'm not threatening you." Instinctively, she lowered her

49

voice and held her head down. "I'm just saying…Matthew."

"Matthew? Matthew what? Told you to tell me that? I will kick that niggas ass. Don't you ever bring that nigga up to me, do you understand me?"

His hand moved to her throat so quick she didn't have time to react. Kayla started banging on the door.

He released her and she turned and opened the door quickly.

"Kevin. I'll pick her up around three."

"I'll let you know when to come by to get her," he said, while opening the front door and pushing her through it. Her mind was racing as she turned from the door and headed back to the car. She didn't want to leave her but she needed Kevin to see that raising a teenage girl wasn't as simple as he thought it was.

Matthew started asking the question before she was fully in the car. "Do you plan on telling me what happened?"

"There is nothing to tell."

"First of all, let me tell you something, I don't like being lied to."

"What have I lied about?"

"Are you honestly going to sit there and tell me that he didn't man handle you again?"

Cheryl remained silent.

"You don't have anything to say?"

"You don't know how it is." She said almost so low he didn't hear her.

"Then tell me how it is!"

He saw her flinch and immediately regretted it. "I'm, sorry. I don't mean to yell. How are you going to lie to me? I told you, I don't like to be lied to. That is one thing that I will not stand for. Do you understand me?"

"Please, don't do this, I am not lying. I just don't want to discuss it right now."

"When will you feel like discussing it?"

"Soon," she said as she touched his hand.

They pulled up in front of her home a few minutes later. "Are you coming in?"

"No, I have something I need to do. I will be back in a little while."

As he drove he made a few calls and pulled into the parking lot of the gym.

"What's up nigga? Why don't I ever hear from you when you don't want to spar?"

"You know I love ya," Matthew said and gave him a slap on the back. "Let me get changed, I'll be right out."

After sparring with David for almost two hours, he felt better. He should have been angry at Cheryl for lying to him but her way of coping with the abuse was to lie to everyone around her.

Chapter 9

After having one more drink, Kevin went to the stairs and called his daughter down.

"Kayla, Rebecca is coming over, and I want you to be on your best behavior."

"I'm not a baby, dad. I know,"

"I told you not to speak to me that way," he said while walking up on her. "I don't know what your mother is teaching you."

"Nothing. Dang, if you…"

"What did you just say?"

"Nothing," Kayla said while stomping into the kitchen. Before she could reach the refrigerator, he had slapped her in the back of the head.

"Don't touch me!" she screamed. "This is bull…"

"Who do you think you are talking to, young lady?"

"You! You don't have to always be hitting on us. You get on my nerves."

"Don't you ever speak to me like that again, do you hear me?"

"Get off of me! I'm calling mom," she yelled.

"Go to your room and don't touch that fucking phone!"

He walked upstairs to Kayla's room and heard her crying.
He blew out a breath. Nothing irritated him more than a

woman crying.

"Kayla, can I come in?"

"Your house."

"Kayla, I think you should stay here for a couple of weeks. I don't know what your mother has been telling you, but I want us to get closer."

Kevin moved closer to her bed and sat down. She moved away.

"Kayla, look. You are a little too young to have such an attitude problem. What is wrong? You can tell me."

"Dad, why you always got to be so mean to mom?"

"Your mother is always blaming me for things and sometimes she pushes me too far. You know some people have limits and you have to know when not to cross them."

"You said that we should never fight but the two of you are always fighting."

"Look Kayla that is none of your concern. Why don't you get dressed and when Rebecca gets here, we will go out to get something to eat?"

"I don't want to," Kayla said while rolling her eyes.

"This isn't a choice. So get dressed and I don't want to hear anything else about it."

Chapter 10

Cheryl felt her phone vibrate but she was giving her order at the seafood counter.

"Yes, the shrimp look good today," she told George, her favorite worker behind the counter.

He smiled at her and said, "You should really cook them yourself. It isn't that hard to do."

"Yes, I know, but tonight is a special occasion and I really just want to take the easy way."

"I guess your husband is a lucky man to have such a pretty wife making dinner for him."

"Oh, George, you're so cute. I'm not married, just fixing dinner for a friend,"

She noticed the guy that was at the counter walked away when she did.

"Can I suggest that you pair your shrimp with a red wine? One that is not dry, but mellow."

"Thank you for the suggestion and have a nice night." She said to the stranger with the patch on his eye.

Before exiting the store, she looked around. Not sure why but she had an uneasy feeling and dismissed it as her nerves being frayed after dealing with Kevin earlier

She got home and checked her phone. She saw that she had a message from Matthew and smiled at his voice.

Rebecca called out when she got into the foyer.

She walked up the stairs and heard him talking to his daughter. God knows Rebecca tried to be civil to the little brat, but her mother had poisoned her mind against her. Rebecca walked back down the stairs when she heard him tell her to get dressed. She went into his office and poured herself a glass of wine.

"Hey sexy."

"Hey yourself. I used my key. I hope you don't mind."

"That's the reason I gave it to you. You know, you could just stay…"

"Let's not start that again," she said while stepping past him.

"Ok, ok. Hope you don't mind, but Kayla is coming with us to dinner. Her mother let her go to one of her little friends' houses last night and they went out and got caught by the police for violating the curfew laws. After that little stunt, I have called the lawyer and told him I want an emergency custody hearing. She is only fifteen years old and there is no way I am going to have her out here running wild." He said as he poured himself a glass of wine.

"Do you think that is wise, now that you have all three of the offices open? Between coming to Atlanta and then going to the office in New York, who will be home with her?"

"Look, I'll cross that bridge when I come to it. Right now her dumb ass mother has her out here running wild. Kayla come on!" he yelled.

"I haven't taken my shower yet," she yelled down.

"Hurry the hell up! You have thirty minutes! God! She is just like her mother, always waiting until the last damn minute."

"Look, just relax. I could think of something we could do for thirty minutes," Rebecca said as she walked behind him and put her hands around his waist. Kevin turned around and embraced her.

"Mmmm, it's been a while since we had any alone time," she cooed in his ear.

"Well, we are alone right now, aren't we?" He said.

She licked his lips and guided his hands under her skirt.

"You seem a little horny, Ms. Hardy."

She didn't say anything, instead she reached inside his trousers and felt his manhood. She started to bend down, but he turned her and bent her over his mahogany desk.

"I want you right now, Rebecca." he growled in her ear, and with that he pushed himself into her.

He entered into her so hard, that he sucked his name from her mouth.

"You feel so good," he moaned in her ear.

She pushed him away, turned and lay back on the desk and pulled him down and he entered her again.

She wrapped her legs around his waist, pulling him deeper inside of her.

"Oh, my god!" She moaned.

The moans and groans filled the space and bounced back at them. They released simultaneously and he rolled onto his back. They both stared at the ceiling

When he was able to stand, he said "What are you trying to do to me?" and finished pulling his pants up.

"Nothing baby, I just needed you. Let's hurry up and eat, because I want more of this," she said while pulling her skirt down. Just then Kayla came knocking on the door.

"Now, I'm waiting on you." Kayla said from behind the door

He swung the door open and gave her a nasty look as he went upstairs. Rebecca grabbed her purse and went into the bathroom as her phone rang. By the time she hung up, she was irritated.

They were finally heading to dinner after an hour. As they walked into McCormick's and Schmitz Kayla stomped her feet, sucked her breath and answered Rebecca rudely whenever she tried to ask her a question.

"Can you stop talking to me? You're here with him, not me." Kayla said moving around Rebecca.

"What in the hell is wrong with you?" Kevin asked as Kayla sat down hard in on the chair in the lobby of the restaurant.

"I don't like this place. I thought we were going out for Chinese or pizza."

"I didn't say anything about Chinese or pizza. This is where Rebecca and I were planning on coming, so this is where we are eating."

"If I knew that, then I wouldn't have come," Kayla said nastily.

"Don't you dare come out of the mouth like that to me, do you understand me?" he said to her while grabbing her upper arm. She tried snatching free of him, but he held her arm harder. "You better settle your fast ass down. Now get yourself together before I…"

"What? Hit me like you do mom?"

"Kayla, that is just about enough."

The waiter came over to announce that their table was ready. Kayla stomped ahead of Kevin and Rebecca.

"Maybe we should just…" Rebecca started to say.

"No, I planned on taking you to dinner and her ass better get it together, or I will get it together for her."

Kayla pulled out her chair, sat down and folded her arms. Kevin pulled out Rebecca's chair as she sat next to Kayla and he sat across from them. Kayla rolled her eyes a couple of times, and he gave her a look that told her to get it together. She put her hands down and picked up her menu. As he was talking to the waiter about wine, Kayla got up and went to the restroom. Dinner was uneventful, especially since Kayla only ordered a salad and was done before his steak had gotten to the table.

As dinner wore on, Rebecca decided to bring up the subject

of a new office manager.

"Kevin, now that we have all of the offices open. Don't you think it is time to hire a new manager for the office here? I have been thinking…"

"Have you? Because I didn't really think we would need one. Ashley is still here and knows the office procedures and the new temp secretary is working out great. I don't think we should put someone in there that would have to be trained."

"Well, that's what I have been thinking. I have the perfect person. I know that she is a hard worker and that she also knows our business. She is a friend that I have known for years, and she just fell on some hard times and I was hoping that maybe you would give her a shot."

"What are her qualifications?"

"She graduated from WVSU with a degree in management. She has lived in New York for about 5 years, but she is looking to relocate."

"I don't know. I hadn't planned on paying for anybody to relocate."

"Don't be so cheap."

Kevin shot her a look.

"I only mean, if you want someone good, you have to be willing to show them that you are serious and that K & B Alliance is not some nickel and dime company."

"You sound very sure of this woman. What is her name?"

"Her name is Antonia, but I call her Toni."

"Well, let's set up an interview. I am not promising you anything, but if she is the good, you know I will hold you personally responsible for her."

"You won't regret it. I will call her tomorrow."

Chapter 11

"I picked up some seafood and your favorite fruit, strawberries," she said as she opened the door to Matthew

"Have you spoken to Kayla since we dropped her off?"

"Briefly, she said they were going out to eat and she didn't want to go because Rebecca was also going."

"Well, baby, she is going to have to get used it to, after all, they are engaged."

"Don't remind me."

"Oh, jealous are we?" Matthew said as he wrapped his arms around her waist.

"Are you kidding me? I'm mad. He made her the head of the new office, when he knew I would give anything to work with him, hell, even as a damn secretary, but he always told me that I needed to be home with the kids. I guess I couldn't..."

"He didn't know what he had. Good thing for me though, because I will never let you forget how important you are to me. Cheryl, put the plates in the oven warmer." He said as he kissed her neck and his hands moved from her hips to her breasts.

"Matthew..."

"Shh, don't say anything." He pulled her to the living room quickly. "Just lay here and let me take care of you."

He laid her down on the carpet and quickly removed his shirt and pulled his pants down. He pulled her nipple to his mouth as he let his fingers slide past her panties and entered her wetness.

"Oh Matthew," she whispered in his ear.

Their release came fast and hard. Her hands scratched his back as his hands found her hair, grabbing a handful, his face buried into the side of her neck. He rolled off of her and she curled up next to him. He welcomed the comfort of feeling her arm drape across his body. As he felt her breathing slow down, he heard a small snore escape from her. He pushed his hand through her hair and kissed her head as a smile swept across his face and he let sleep take him into its embrace.

Matthew's cell phone rang, breaking his sex induced nap. He picked it up without looking at the display.

"Hello."

"Tired? I guess she wore you out, huh?" The husky voice said.

He sat up and Cheryl rolled off lazily. "Who is this?" he whispered.

"I already answered that question before, so stop asking it, it's getting a little old." The man said.

"Look, I don't know who the fuck this is, but if I find..."

"Don't make me laugh. I will come for you soon enough. Did you enjoy the shrimp that your lady friend picked up tonight? I sure hope she took my suggestion and got the red wine." The line went dead and he nudged Cheryl.

"Cheryl?" He nudged her awake.

She stretched her long legs and looked up his face.

Sorry, I fell asleep. Thank you for that. I guess you have worked up quite an appetite, huh?"

She got up and went into the bathroom. She talked from behind the door.

"I picked up some red wine. I am not sure if you will like it, but..."

He dropped the glass, "Did you say red wine? Did the butcher recommend it?"

"No, actually it was another customer…"

"Look, don't go talking to everyone in the store. You never…"

"Are you serious?" she asked him as she walked out and towards the kitchen. "Don't worry, I didn't give him my number, although…."

He cut her off, "Look, just don't get too friendly with the people in the store."

Cheryl flinched as he walked up to her.

"Sorry, I didn't mean to sound like that…but you have to be careful."

"No problem, he seemed nice enough, although he got a little creepy at the end."

"What do you mean?"

"Just that he kept following me around the store. Probably was just lonely or something."

"What did he look like?"

"Um, average. Might have been about forty or fifty years old. Funny thing, he had a decent body, kind of like he lifted weights or something. Nothing compared to you though," she said while pressing a kiss onto his cheek.

"What else did he look like? Was he black, white, Puerto…"

"Look, no big deal."

His phone buzzed signaling a text message coming through. He looked at the screen and read:

See, even she didn't care enough to find out who I was…
No worries, soon enough you both will know exactly who I am.

After another session of intense love making, Matthew stood

and pulled Cheryl up with him. He kissed her face as she padded upstairs and he went to the bathroom down the hall. He was in the living room and picked up his phone.

"Look Tyrone, I need you to try and trace all incoming calls to my phone and also I want it done for my office phones....not sure what is going on but I intend to find out."

Just then Cheryl's phone rang as she rounded the corner. She picked it up and slammed it back down

"What's wrong?" He asked when he looked into her face.

"Nothing."

"Are you sure?"

"Yes."

The phone rang again.

"Are you going to get it?" He asked her as she stared at the phone. After the third ring she answered but immediately hung up.

They arrived at the door to the house she used to call home with Kevin and a moment of nostalgia struck her. She remembered the first time she stood on those steps. She shook the memory from her head and rang the bell.

"What in the hell are you doing here?" Kevin said when he flung the door open.

She walked past him and called for Kayla

"I am not going to ask you again." He grabbed her arm just as Kayla came running down the steps.

Cheryl gasped as she saw the semi-circle scratch on the side of her daughter's face.

"You hit her!" Cheryl's voice was more of a screech than a yell.

"I slapped her because she has a nasty mouth. Something I am sure she has gotten from you."

"I'm calling..." but his hand on her throat cut off the words.

Rebecca appeared at the top of the steps and he relaxed his grip.

"I want to go home." Kayla said

"Kevin, since I am already here..." Cheryl interrupted.

"No one told you to come over here."

"Kayla called me. I'm taking her home," she said while reaching for her daughter's hand.

"I said she is not going anywhere!" He shoved Cheryl against the door and she let out a small scream.

Rebecca moved to his side and pulled his hands away from Cheryl.

"Kayla, go get in the car. I'll be right out."

She spoke to Rebecca, "I hope you never have to endure this. Now you see how he really is."

"I can handle my man just fine." Rebecca said as she walked towards the office.

Kevin appeared again and pinned her against the door frame.

"Kevin, take your hands off of me."

"Yeah, I suggest you take your hands off of her," Matthew said as he stepped into the open doorway.

Kevin pushed Cheryl towards Matthew and Cheryl put her hand against Matthew's chest to keep him from going back inside.

"Keep that mothafucka out of my house. The next time, I won't be so nice," Kevin shouted as they were leaving.

"I'll tell you this. The next time you think about putting your fucking hands on Cheryl, the coroner will have to be called to pick up the pieces of your sorry ass."

Matthew was pacing in the driveway when Cheryl walked out. Kayla was standing next to the car with her arms folded.

"Cheryl, if I had not come in there, God only knows what he would have done to you."

As they pulled up in front of Cheryl's townhouse, Matthew

thought he saw something from the corner of his eye. He told them to wait in the car as he got out.

Kevin was pacing around the living room like a caged animal.

"Look, I'm sorry you had to see that."

"Why do you let her do that?"

"Do what?"

"Push your buttons like that. She ran over here just because you had to discipline your daughter, then she brings her little boyfriend over here with her. You then let her talk to you…"

"Wait a damn minute. I didn't allow her to talk to me no kind of way. Secondly, this is none of your fucking business," he shouted.

"Who in the hell do you think you are talking to? Nigga, I ain't Cheryl."

"Don't you ever question me," he yelled while running up on her.

"Who do you think you are?" she said as she pushed him away from her, "Let me say this, if you ever *think* about putting your damn hands on me, it will be last thing you do."

"What the fuck is that supposed to mean?" He said while walking behind her, grabbing her by the arm.

"Just what the hell I said….don't you ever put your hands on me like that!" She yelled as she stormed back upstairs and slammed the bedroom door.

Chapter 12

"Matthew, is that a gun? What in the hell is going on?"

"Nothing. I carry it for protection." He said, "I thought I asked you to stay in the car."

"I don't like guns, and would prefer that you not carry it when we are together." She said as she unlocked the front door

"That won't happen," he said. They walked in and he noticed that she walked past the alarm system. "Did you set the alarm?"

"I keep forgetting. Kevin used to get on me all the time about that when we lived together."

"Look, you and Kayla are living here by yourselves. You need to be a little more careful. Although you live in the suburbs, crime can happen anywhere. I can't have anything happening to the both of you."

"Matthew, how long have you carried a gun?"

"I don't know…years, when you live the kind of life that I did, you needed to protect yourself."

"Well, when you are here, can you not carry it? Or at the very least, not let me see it."

Monday came and Rebecca walked into Kevin's office.

"Toni will be up shortly. Should I have the assistant show her around?"

Kevin was sitting behind his mahogany desk."Yes, give her the questionnaire and have her wait." He got up and walked in front of his desk. "Close the door, Rebecca, How long before she arrives?" He said while walking over to her and pulling her close

"Hmm, I think…" she said, not returning his embrace.

"That long huh?" he said.

Suddenly there was a knock on the door.

"Yes Ashley."

"Ms. Antonia Downs is here."

"Thank you, have her wait for one minute,"

He walked back over to his desk and straightened his tie. Kevin paged Ashley to let her know she could bring in Ms. Downs.

As she entered, he extended his hand to the chocolate woman standing in front of him. She had on a cream colored pant suit that highlighted her skin color and her hair was cut very short. Her eyes were a light green and the ring in her nose was a bit off putting.

Thank you again, Rebecca, for setting me up with this interview. I promise you, Mr. Goldman, that you will not be sorry."

"Oh, but I haven't hired you yet."

"But you will."

By the end of the week, Cheryl was feeling worn down. She woke up feeling dizzy and had a slight fever. Her son, Donnell, said he was coming into town tonight and she ordered a catered dinner to be delivered around seven. Matthew had to work late so he wouldn't be able to attend.

Since he wasn't going to join them for dinner, Cheryl took lunch to his office, but his secretary told her he would be in a meeting all afternoon, so she left the food and a note.

She went home and climbed into the shower hoping it would make her feel better. She pressed on when the caterers arrived at six. She was thankful that she didn't have to do anything because she was starting to feel worse and worse.

The doorbell rang and she opened it to see her son standing there. She hadn't realized she had missed him as much as she had. He moved out immediately after graduating and hadn't been back for three years.

"Ma."

"Donnell. How is my baby?"

"Fine ma. Are you going to invite me in?"

"Oh, sorry. Yes, come in here boy and let me get a good look at you."

"Ma. I am not a boy..."

"Yes, you are, you will always be my little boy." She pulled him towards the living room and pulled him down on the sofa beside her. "Now tell me what you have been up to."

"So, this is your place...nice. I guess the man you divorced did something right."

"Donnell..."

"Ok, sorry...well I aint been up to nothing much. I found a job down in North Carolina so after I graduate from grad school, I'll be moving down there with Danielle."

"Moving to North Carolina. Why?"

"Mom, there is nothing in Salisbury or here..."

"I'm here, Kayla's here, your dad..."

"Dad and I aren't talking since..."

She interrupted him, "Look, why don't we eat first, we can talk about it after dinner, when is Danielle coming?" "She should be here soon."

"Ok, I can't wait to meet her."

"I can't wait for you to meet her either. I think you are going to love her just like I do."

"My baby is in love. Is there a wedding on the horizon?" she asked as she disappeared into the kitchen to get the bottle of wine.

Cheryl heard the doorbell from the kitchen and Donnell told her he would get it. She turned as she heard her son's footsteps behind her and the clicking of heels on the hardwood floor.

"Mom, I want you to meet Danielle."

She turned and saw her son holding the hands of a very tall young woman. She had to be as tall as him and had high cheekbones. Her eyes were those of Asian descent but her olive color suggested mixed heritage. Her silky hair was curled and her full lips were accented with a hint of lip gloss. Since he had only brought home two or three girls, this one was definitely the prettiest.

"Nice meeting you."

She smiled at her son.

"Mom, we need to tell you something."

"Am I having a grandbaby?"

"What? Are you serious?" He laughed, "Mom, really. No."

"Well there is nothing else that you need to tell me." She walked back into the kitchen and felt a wave of nausea sweep over her. She took a deep breath, closed her eyes and picked up the tray of food.

She walked in and sat the tray in front of the couple.

"Mom, why do you always go to the extreme? I told you I just wanted dinner, not a party."

"Boy, hush. This ain't no party, this is your dinner. You better eat up." She started laughing.

"I think I'm going to like her," Danielle said as she popped a grape into her mouth.

They shared a laugh as Cheryl sat down beside Donnell, grabbed his hand and gave it a squeeze.

He whispered in her ear. "Thanks"

"For what?" she asked

"Just thanks." He said as he leaned in and hugged her. He

drew back and put his hand on her cheek.

"Mom you feel ok? You feel a little warm."

"Aww isn't that cute, you trying to be my mother." she said. As she stood, the phone rang.

"Let me grab this and I will be right back."

"Hello." She said into the receiver.

"Hello sexy. I am hoping that dinner tastes as good as you looked."

"Who is this?" she said as she turned her back to the crowd sitting in the living room.

"Don't worry about who this is, worry about when I'm going to come for you."

"Look, I don't know…"

"Why not ask your little boyfriend who I am. He knows me very well. Better yet, give him a message for me.

Cheryl's words wouldn't come as she felt the tightness begin.

The voice continued, "let Matthew know that I plan on taking my time with you. I plan on tasting every inch."

She slammed the phone down and the room began to spin.

Cheryl's chest tightened and she tried to gain control of her breathing, but it wasn't working and her inhaler was upstairs. The pressure became intense and she began coughing. She looked up as Donnell approached and her heart started beating rapidly. Her eyes blinked rapidly as she began to call her son's name.

Her eyes fluttered open as the faces came into focus. Donnell helped her into a sitting position.

"Mom, you fainted. I told you that you felt warm earlier, has your asthma been acting up again. I thought you had it under control. "

Matthew's words rushed out at her after Donnell's. "Did Kevin call you? Did he threaten you? I swear to god if that…"

"When did you get here?" she said with her eyebrows frowned.

"I've been here for almost ten minutes." He said as he wrapped his arm around her shoulder. "Who was on the phone?"

"I don't know who it was. He said something about seeing me soon and to stop asking who it was. My asthma has been acting up all day. I should have given myself a treatment. I am sorry to have caused all of this trouble."

"No big deal. Mom, what if we weren't here? What if you were by yourself and hit your head or something? ".

"Come on. Let's get you up to bed to rest." Matthew said while helping her to stand.

"I will not. Donnell came all the way here for dinner with Danielle and I am not disappointing him. Besides I made his favorites."

"You made barbequed pork chops?"

"Ok, well I didn't make them but someone did. Besides, I have all your favorites and I even picked up a strawberry cheesecake."

"That's what's up," Donnell said as he walked into the kitchen.

"See how he gets when there is food involved. He forgets all about me," Danielle said.

"Baby, no I don't," Donnell said while walking back to her and wrapping his arms around her. "You know I could never forget about you."

It wasn't until Matthew cleared his throat that they remembered they weren't alone.

Chapter 13

Rebecca threw her purse on the couch and started disrobing as she walked throughout her house, heading to the shower. She faintly heard the door and then her phone rang again. She threw open the shower door and headed into the living room with a towel wrapped around her but it did nothing for the water she was trailing behind her.

"Wait a minute. Let me get there first!" She yelled while pulling open the door.

"What are you doing here this late? Why didn't you call first?" she asked as he brushed past her.

"The same reason you didn't answer my calls, I didn't feel like it, where have you been?" Kevin asked as he snatched her purse from the couch.

"I told you, I went by my parents' house and had a few other errands to run."

"Really?" he asked as he walked towards her bedroom. "So why didn't you answer my calls?"

"Kevin, is this why you came over here, to give me the third degree? If so, I am not in the mood for it and we can discuss this on Monday." She said from behind him.

"So, you aren't going to tell me where you were tonight?"

She noticed his words were slurred, "I already told you."

"No, you said you were at your parents' house which we both know is a lie. I drove by there and didn't see your car"

"So you are checking up on me. Look this ring doesn't give you the right…"

He turned and slapped her hard, sending her stumbling back a couple of steps.

"Don't you ever fucking talk to me that way again, do you understand me?"

"Who the fuck do you think you are? Don't you ever put your fucking hands on me." she yelled as she lunged for him.

He caught her hand in mid swing and slapped her again.

"Get out. Get the fuck out of my house." She screamed.

"I will leave when I'm fucking ready," he said calmly while walking out to her living room and sitting down.

"Kevin, so help me, if you don't leave, I'll call the police." She said as she stomped behind him.

"Will you…I don't think so. Rebecca, you do remember who I am? If Cheryl couldn't do anything to me, do you think you will? Now sit your fucking ass down and tell me where you have been." He said.

"I think you better go," Rebecca said while holding the towel tight around her.

"And I think you better sit your ass down like I told you a second ago."

"Kevin, look. It's late and I am not in the mood…"

He stood and closed the distance between them before she finished the sentence.

"Rebecca, don't fucking play with me, hear? I am not in the mood for your lying. Now you will tell me where you have been or so help me, you will regret it."

"I went to my parent's house and then picked up my dry cleaning."

"Until two in the fucking morning?" He said while tightening his grip.

"No. Then I went by Toni's house and we had a few drinks

and talked about old times. I lost track of time and I didn't hear my phone because it was in my purse."

"See, that's all you had to say. If I ask you something all you have to do is tell me. Understand?" he said as he pulled his hand away from her neck.

He sat down on the sofa and motioned for her to sit next to him. She stood in her same spot, her hand rubbing her neck.

"Now don't be that way. You could have prevented all of this if you would have called and told me that, instead you had me calling you and waiting hours for you. Now, come here. You know you want this." He said as his hand grabbed the front of his pants.

"Kevin, I'm not in the mood." She said as she readjusted the towel.

"But you will be." He said as he got up and went over to her. He kneeled in front of her and began kissing her knee, then her leg, then her thigh.

"Kevin, stop," she said as she rolled her eyes to the top of her head.

"Let me make it up to you," he said while he continued kissing her.

She pushed his shoulders away and stepped back.

"You need to leave."

"What?" he said as he wiped his mouth and stood in front of her.

"You heard me. Leave."

"Rebecca. What are you talking about?"

"Kevin, you heard me.

"You're joking, right?"

"Do I look like I'm fucking joking? I told you that I am not Cheryl and you will not put your goddamn hands on me."

"Look, I'm sorry. I was mad." He said as he reached for her.

"I don't give a...."

"Look, calm down. It aint that serious."

She laughed out the words "are you serious?"

"Yes I am serious. It is not a big deal."

"Get out!" she yelled while walking quickly to the front door.

He walked over and snatched her hand away from the door before she could open it.

"Bitch, you better lower your fucking voice. I'm tired and I am not going anywhere." He said as he walked away from the door, started removing his clothes and walked upstairs.

Chapter 14

Matthew got to his office and Bo, his friend for years, was already there.

"Look, I need to know who the fuck is calling my lady. If it's that ex-husband of hers, I swear to god I will slit his throat and feed him to the dogs."

"Damn, I haven't seen you like this in quite some time."

"Man, I told her I would always protect her and I meant every word of it. She has been through years of shit and she is not going to go through that again."

"Nigga, I'm straight. The real question is does Terry know about this part of your past?"

"Nope and he never will," he said as he sat down beside his friend. "First I need to find out where this call came from." He showed Bo the number he had gotten from Cheryl's phone. "Can you call your contact at the phone company?"

"Just give me a few minutes," Bo said as he motioned for him to get up. Matthew paced around his office until Bo yelled 'got it' and turned the computer screen for Matthew to see it. Matthew let out a stream of curse words and grabbed his keys from the desk.

"What are you going to do?"

"I'm going to deal with it," he said and stormed out.

"Open this fucking door!" Matthew yelled while pounding on

the red door.

"What in the hell do you want?" Sherrie asked while pulling the door open.

He grabbed her and shoved her into the wall of the foyer.

"I'm only going to ask you one fucking time, and you better tell me the fucking truth. Why are you calling and harassing Cheryl...did you actually believe I wouldn't find out it was you?"

"Get your fucking hands off of me!" Sherrie said while pushing around him, "I don't know what you are talking about."

"Don't fucking lie to me!" He said as he grabbed her and spun her around.

Her eyes grew large. "I'm not! I swear."

He released her arms, "Look, somebody has been calling me and Cheryl and it is freaking her out."

"Well, that's what you get for getting involved with someone that has a crazy ass ex-husband. No telling what that nigga would do."

Donell opened the door and let Matthew in. He was immediately hit with questions.

"Care to tell me what in the hell is going on?" Donnell said.

"I am not sure myself. Where is Cheryl?" Matthew said walking past Donnell.

"What does that mean, you're not sure?"

"Donnell, trust me when I tell you, I am going to find out who it is, and when I do...How's your mom?"

"She is finally calm, if that is what you mean."

"Is she ok?"

"Yeah, she finally fell asleep, but wanted me to wake her up when you got here."

Matthew told him not to do that as Donnell headed for the stairs. "You two should get some rest."

Donnell came back down the two steps and stood in front of Matthew.

"Thanks for loving my mom and showing her that she is actually worth it," Donnell said before grabbing his girlfriend's hand and walking upstairs.

Matthew walked into Cheryl's room and saw her curled in a ball, He lay down beside her and she opened her eyes and tried sitting up.

"Lie back down and sleep. I'm here now." he said and wrapped his arms around her. He drifted to sleep after a while. Her snores pulled him awake and he pulled his gun from his leg and placed it on the nightstand. As he fell into a half sleep, he thought, *better safe than sorry.*

Chapter 15

"Morning beautiful." Kevin said when he walked in and saw Rebecca standing in his office with a black long skirt and form fitting jacket. She had diamond earrings in her ears but a little too much makeup for his taste.

"A little too much makeup this morning." He commented while walking behind his desk and putting his briefcase down.

Rebecca moved closer to him, "Are you serious? You are going to act like you don't..."

Kevin interrupted her, "What is on the agenda today?" He said without looking up.

Rebecca drew in a breath and mumbled.

"Got something else to say?" Kevin said as he looked up at her.

"Well, Toni starts today and we have that meeting with the Alpine Spa and Hotel àgain. You know they signed with M & T Limos and now they are looking for a public relations company to promote the new management. At noon we have that lunch meeting with Greg from the bank and we have the three o'clock meeting with Corey and the partners in New York."

"So when do we get alone time?"

"Not today."

"What is wrong with you?"

"Did you forget what happened on Saturday?"

He blew out a breath of air, " I thought we had talked about that already. What's the matter now?" he said as he walked towards his mini bar and poured himself some grapefruit juice. She walked towards him and crossed her arms in front of herself. He brushed by her and sat behind his desk.

"The problem is, I am not Cheryl and you will not...let me repeat that. You will not put your fucking hands on me. Do you understand me?"

She pulled a slip of paper from her pocket and threw it on his desk.

"His name is Detective Brown. I called him on Sunday and asked him the procedures for filing a police report for domestic violence. He told me what I would need to do. So if you ever think about putting your hands on me again, remember this, you will sit your black ass in jail! Do I make myself clear?"

She righted herself, pulled her jacket down and walked out of his office just as his desk phone rang.

He ended the call just as Ashley came in with four pages of information on M & T Limo Company. The original owner had gotten into some hot water with the IRS and had taken on another partner about five years ago. There wasn't much information on the M part of the M & T Limo, so he would need to dig a little deeper. He made more calls, but the conversation with Rebecca played in the back of his mind. It didn't help his mood that Corey was late for their meeting.

"Hey nigga. What's up?" Corey said as he pushed open the oak door and walked into Kevin's office.

"You were supposed to be here over an hour ago. I told you to make sure you were here by eleven. It is after twelve and you waltz in here, acting like you in the club."

"What the hell is the problem? I'm here, aren't I? Anyway I told you last night that I would be late. Did you forget you had me out at the club half the night?"

As he sat down, Kevin walked up on him "Don't fucking get cute. I'm not in the mood,"

"What the fuck is your problem?" Corey said while standing to his full six foot height.

"The problem is you don't know when to be on fucking time," Kevin said while pointing his finger in Corey's face.

"What the fuck is this shit?" he said while slapping his hand away.

Kevin's words tumbled from his mouth, "I'm tired of your lazy attitude. I told you to be here at a certain time and you act like I said it for the fun of it."

"Nigga it ain't that serious," he said while stepping back.

"Nigga you better slow your roll," Kevin said as he stepped further into Corey's personal space.

"Look I'm here, besides I don't see 'ole girl here." He said looking around.

"We aren't talking about Rebecca."

"Why not? If I'm supposed to be on time, so is she," he said, raising his voice.

"What the fuck did you just say to me?"

"Nigga, you better back the fuck down, I know you aint running up on me."

"You want to go there?" Kevin said, spit landing on Corey's face.

"Nigga, you better remember who the fuck you are dealing with, I aint Cheryl, so you better back the fuck up."

A knock and the door opening, interrupted the words about to come out of Kevin's mouth. Ashley had the habit of knocking and walking before being *invited* in.

Ashley waited until Corey left the office.

"Rough morning, huh?" she said.

"What do you want?"

"I have the information you wanted."

"Are you going to tell me or not." He half yelled .

"Dang, you don't have to bite my head off. Well, after digging a little deeper, I was able to find that M and T Limo is actually owned by Mr. Matthew Perry and…"

"Shit!" he said as he pushed all of the contents from his desk onto the floor.

Ashley stared at him before he yelled at her to get out of his office.

As Cheryl walked towards her living room she heard a heated discussion between Donnell and Danielle.

"I said I would tell her, now stop bugging me about it. Shit!"

"Stop stalling and tell her. We are not getting married until you do. Do you want her hearing it from someone else?''

"Hell no, but you aren't going to pressure me into doing it either," Donnell said as he walked away from her.

"I am not pressuring you. Your father knows and hasn't said shit to you ever since. Your mother seems cool and you are keeping it from her. That ain't right, Donnell. You said you would tell her and now you are backing out. If you want us to be together than you better tell her."

Donnell poured juice in his glass as he spoke, "Again, I will tell her when I am ready to tell her, not when you tell me."

"Seriously, you need to get a grip and stop giving orders, like your father."

Donnell grabbed Danielle. "Don't you ever say that to me! Do you hear me? Don't you ever compare me to that son of a bitch! I am nothing like him, nothing!" He let Danielle go and she ran out of the kitchen.

Cheryl walked over to her son. "What did you do to her?
"Nothing."

"She didn't run out of her for nothing son."

"We had a little disagreement that's all mom, I'm sorry."

81

"I'm not the one you should be saying that to. Whatever you need to tell me can wait, Danielle can't."

Chapter 16

Corey, Rebecca and Kevin arrived at the restaurant around one fifteen. Rebecca had suggested that Toni come along, Kevin vetoed that as soon as it left her mouth.

"Good afternoon. Have you been waiting long?" Kevin addressed Scott and Santana, his business partners, sitting at the table.

Suddenly Kevin's jaw clenched.

"What is wrong with you?" She asked.

"You will see in a few minutes." He said as he pulled her chair out for her.

When the waiter arrived, Kevin ordered a double cognac.

"What do you think you are doing?" Corey asked.

"Mind your fucking business." Kevin whispered as he sat back.

Terry and Matthew walked in and were led to the table by the waitress.

The older gentleman began the introductions. "Kevin Goldman, let me introduce you to…"

"I already know Mr. Perry…let's get this meeting underway, shall we? I don't have all day." Kevin said as he swallowed the last of his drink.

After two hours of non-stop talk, Kevin spoke up, "So let me get this straight. You want us to not only represent you but also

83

this limo company, for one flat rate? It seems to me that if the limo service wanted representation, they would pay for it themselves."

Matthew spoke up "Had we known of the intentions of Scott and Santana, we might have thought about it, but hey, we know a deal when we see one."

Kevin's jaw got tight. "Oh, I see. It's about being cheap. It figures someone like you would want something for nothing."

Terry interrupted, "It's not just a limo service. We have certified drivers and we also offer other amenities with our car service."

"Like what? Driving home women and taking advantage of them?"

"I don't know what you are talking about," Matthew answered Kevin.

Santana spoke up, "Gentleman, seems like we have gotten off track. Is there a problem we should know about?"

Corey spoke up quickly while shooting a side eye at Kevin, "No. There is not a problem that can't be solved. Let's look at the numbers again, and then we can give you our answer."

"Good. I don't have all day to spend on this, and trust me, we can find another PR firm if necessary." Scott said.

Rebecca and Corey both shot Kevin a look.

Kevin finally said. "Shall we toast? I think we will have a great partnership," he said as he raised his glass and not waiting for anyone, gulped down the amber liquid, sitting his empty glass down. They parted company as Cheryl walked towards the table.

She walked confidently into the restaurant and was led to the table with her ex-husband, her current beau and friends she hadn't seen in a while. Instantly her confidence was gone.

She spoke first. "Good afternoon Santana and Scott, how are

you doing today?" she said as she made her way to them and they rose and each gave her a hug.

"Matthew didn't tell me you were joining us." Santana said.

Kevin spoke up quickly. "Why would she need to be here? After all, this is a business meeting."

"The same reason Rebecca is here." Matthew spoke behind her.

"Hello, handsome, ready for lunch?" Cheryl said.

"You didn't get my message?" Matthew said as he stood.

"I'm sor...I mean, no I didn't, I was saying good bye to Donnell and Danielle. They decided to go to the mountains. Actually I gave them our room for a couple of days. Scott, I hope that was ok," she said, turning to speak to Scott.

"Sure, that's fine. I'll call ahead and make sure they are taken care of." Scott excused himself while Corey and Santana finished talking. Kevin sat as still as an eagle watching his prey.

"I'm a little hungry, I haven't had a chance to eat all day," she said as Matthew continued to stand.

"Where's Kayla?" Kevin said.

"At the house," she said.

"Alone?"

"Yes, alone. She is not a baby, Kevin. She had some homework and a project to do."

"I didn't ask you that" he said while standing.

"Hold on partna. I would suggest you watch the way you talk to my lady."

"Look nigga, this is none of your business. I am talking to her about *my* child."

Cheryl spoke up, "Correction, our child. Look Kevin, first of all, there was a half day of school today. I picked her up and then we had a girl's day. Now she has work to do and coming out for a late lunch wasn't an option for her."

"Again, I didn't ask you that," Kevin shot back.

"I was just telling you." she said back.

"I suggest you sit down, Mr. Goldman," Matthew emphasized his name. "I would hate to ruin my suit fucking with you." He said as he started to pull his jacket off.

Kevin threw the napkin he was holding on the table. "I will talk to you later," he said at her while walking away.

"Matthew, was that necessary?" Cheryl said.

"Yes, it was." Matthew said as he pulled his jacket back up onto his shoulders. "You have no idea what this fucking day has been like. We have been here listening to his bullshit all afternoon. I didn't even know this was the PR firm that Scott was talking about, but they wanted to do business with them and lucky enough, Kevin has some kind of sense because they are now representing Alpine and us."

"I am sure Kevin is not happy about that," she said as she sat down.

Matthew sat down beside her and kissed her hand. "Are you really hungry…for food?" He asked her seductively.

"Yes, I am. Now get your mind out of the gutter." She laughed as the pulled her hand from his and picked up the menu.

Chapter 17

Cheryl got home and helped Kayla finish her project for her history class. Afterwards Cheryl needed to talk to her dad, the one person that always made her feel calm and at peace.

"So now you call?" Cheryl's mother asked her.

"Mom, what is that supposed to mean?"

"Now that you need me, you want to call."

"Mom what are you talking about?" She asked while throwing her head back with her eyes closed.

"Now that Kevin is dragging you back in court, I guess you want me to testify for you," she said.

"Wait, I talk to you every day and you haven't mentioned word of this to me and now you are telling me that you knew this all along. I swear, if I didn't know better I would think YOU were his damn wife." Cheryl screamed as the tears started to stream down her face. She slammed the phone down and called her lawyer.

"Shelly, my mom just told me about a court hearing. Do you know anything about this?"

"Yes, I've been trying to reach you all day. Kevin has called an emergency custody hearing and the judge has granted it."

"Why?"

"All I know is it has something to do with Kayla being left alone and being picked up for violating curfew, something you neglected to tell me."

"Oh my god! Are you serious? This is such crap! When is it?"

"Next Wednesday."

"Seriously?"

"Cheryl I have to tell you, unless you have a good explanation for her being picked up, you just might lose sole custody."

"Oh Hell no! I will not have her staying with him. Absolutely not! I'll call you back." She grabbed her keys from the bar and told Kayla she would be back later. Her mind was all over the place as she drove. She pulled up in front of the house and practically ran to the door.

"Why do you always have to be so hateful?" Cheryl asked as the door opened.

"I know you are not standing at my door making accusations." Kevin said as he turned and walked away from the door.

"Kevin, I will not share custody. You agreed that I could have sole custody with liberal visitation rights. I haven't stopped you from seeing her," she said as she stepped into the house.

"No, but you have her out at all hours of the night, you have her being picked up by the police and you have her around that new nigga of yours."

"She got picked up for being stupid, which might I remind you, does happen to a lot of teenagers. Secondly, I don't like her being out or home alone but I have to work."

"Whatever...you should have thought about that when you started traipsing all around town."

"What about you? I don't say anything about Rebecca, do I? I do believe you're the one traveling all the time, you're the one with the girlfriend spending the night..."

"What I do in my fucking house is none of your business."

"And what I do in my fucking house is none of yours!"

He spun around and grabbed her by the shirt.

"Don't you get cute with me. You thought you were being a smart ass earlier with your little boyfriend."

"Get your damn hands off of me. I should tell them what you did to Kayla the night she got picked up. Seems like the court might not like to hear that you spanked a fifteen year old with a belt, or maybe I should tell them that you...."

He slapped her, hard enough to send her to her knees.

"Stop!" She yelled as she tried to get to her feet.

He grabbed a fistful of hair and pulled her along for a couple of steps.

"Kevin, I'm sorry!" She tried loosening his grip on her hair as he continued sliding her across the hardwood floors.

"Get the fuck out of my house!" He screamed as he pushed her towards the front door. She slapped at his hands again and he slapped her hard enough that it sucked the air from her lungs.

"Don't you ever come here like that, or so help me, you will regret it."

She was breathing heavily as she climbed into her car and drove home. She got home and walked into the house and leaned against the wall.

"Mom, what's wrong?" Kayla asked as she came up to her mother.

"Nothing...except your dad is taking me back to court because you got yourself picked up last week! Now you see why I ask you not do certain things, but you have to always be slick! Now look, you might have to go live with your dad."

Kayla ran upstairs to her room and slammed the door and Cheryl went into her room and laid across the bed.

Cheryl woke up coughing and tried not to get up but it got bad enough that she had to. She walked to the top of the stairs and saw the lights still on in the living room.

"Kayla, can you bring me some water? Kayla!"

She walked downstairs and turned off the television and headed towards the kitchen. She got herself some water and used her inhaler. The clock in the kitchen said ten o'clock.

"Kayla! Kayla!" She called again and went to her room and opened her door. She began to panic and ran and got her cellphone from her purse.

The police arrived just ahead of Kevin.

Cheryl was explaining how she went to bed and Kayla was doing the rest of her homework

"Who is in charge?" Kevin said to the police officer.

"Kevin, I don't know what happened. She was here," she said with bloodshot eyes.

Kevin looked down at her and rolled his eyes and said a few curse words under his breath before speaking to the officer.

"Look, obviously her mother was lying up in bed, doing god knows what…"

"I was not! I wasn't feeling good after leaving you …"

As Matthew spoke to the officer, Kayla walked in asking what was going on.

"Where have you been?" Kevin yelled while walking towards Kayla.

"I just went down the street," she said with a rolling of her eyes.

"Your mom has been worried sick about…" Matthew said.

"Look, I don't need you talking for me," Kevin said to Matthew. "Now answer the damn question."

"Let's give her a chance to tell us," Matthew said while guiding her towards the kitchen to sit down at the table. She sat down and started twirling her hair.

Kevin's face was contorted in such a way that it look like he might pop the vein in the middle of his forehead.

"Like hell I will! You tell us where the fuck you have been!"

Kayla turned towards her mother and spoke, "Mom, I asked you if I could go down to Denise's house to finish up my project. You told me yes."

"I knew your dumb..." Kevin whirled towards Cheryl.

"Ease up partna," Matthew grabbed his arm

Kevin snatched his arm away, "Look, you need to mind your fucking business,"

"Who do you think you are talking to?" Matthew said while walking closer to him.

"Look, nigga. I have had enough of you putting your nose in my business. Like I told the officer, if Cheryl wasn't laying up with you tonight..."

"Correction, she wasn't with me tonight."

"Whatever, she is always doing some dumb shit...."

Cheryl spoke softly, "If I told Kayla she could go, that was my fault. I was tired and half asleep."

"You and your fucking excuses, you are always letting those kids do anything. Look at Donnell's gay ass..."

"Stop calling him that."

"Calling him what, a faggot?"

"He is half yours too, so if I have a faggot for a son, guess what, so do you."

Kevin lunged for her but not before Matthew grabbed him by the shirt and had punched him in the mouth before the officers could get between them.

Kevin spit out the blood and yelled. "Don't you ever put your fucking..."

Cheryl pulled Matthew close to her, "Matthew, please you are only making him upset."

"Really?" he said as he snatched away from her and half laughed "I don't give a rat's ass about making him upset. Tell me one thing though, what happened when you saw him earlier."

Cheryl turned away from him and walked into the living room with the officers just as they escorted Kevin out. After assuring the officers that they would be ok, she shut the door and heard a glass break. She ran towards the kitchen.

Kevin got home and poured himself a drink. He downed one and then quickly poured another one. His doorbell rang and he opened it.

He didn't have time to finish the words as the fight was on.

Matthew's hand connected with the side of his face before Kevin had a chance to react.

The fight spilled into the front yard and Matthew had the advantage when he pulled the gun from his waist and pointed it between Kevin's eyes.

"Put your hands on her again and I'll put a bullet in you." He said as he got up and walked off.

Chapter 18

Matthew poured himself a drink and drank it down. He poured another one and then another.

"You know you shouldn't be drinking like that." Lynette said.

"I don't need you to tell me that." Matthew said without turning around.

"Well, at least let me fix you something."

"No thanks." He said as he downed another one. "Do you want to tell me what happened?"

He sat the glass down and turned around. He looked at the older woman standing in front of him. His housekeeper was more than that, she was someone that he knew he could talk to.

"She let that nigga hit her again. I don't get it, she keeps putting herself in situations with him and then when I try and help her, she gets upset with me."

She spoke quietly as she walked over to him and led him to the chair next to the desk in his office.

"Matthew, now you know I am not one to pry, but you have to remember one thing. This woman has been married to that man for over seventeen years. Sometimes we, meaning women, have a tendency to go towards everything that is wrong in a relationship because that is *all* we know. She doesn't know what it is to be cared for by someone. You said yourself that he has abused her since they first got married. Do you honestly believe that she can forget all of that in the span of a year or two? Give

93

her some time. I am sure she will see what she has."

"I am not going to stand around waiting for her forever," he said as he got up and walked back to the counter, grabbing the bottle and glass.

"Somehow I think you will," she said as he walked out.

Cheryl had to make it right between them. She picked up the phone and dialed.

"Hello."

"How are you feeling?" he asked her.

"Better. Matthew, I am sorry for this evening. I never should have gone over there. I found out some news and I know I should have called you, but I figure I have to learn how to deal with his ass by myself."

"You don't have to deal with him by yourself. I am here to help you." He said as he laid back on his king sized bed.

"I know, but I am a big girl. I have to learn to stand on my own two feet."

"So that means you don't want my help?"

Cheryl laid back on her pillows and began twirling her hair between her fingers. "No that means, you can't fight my battles for me."

"I am not trying to fight them *for* you, I am fighting them *with* you."

"Matthew?"

"Yes sweetness." He said in his deepest voice.

"I love you."

"I love you too." he said.

"Goodnight."

His phone rang again and his face contorted with rage. He looked at the screen, jotted down the number. The call had left Matthew wired and he tossed and turned. He was just about to head to the basement when he heard his doorbell ring. Lynette would be fast asleep in her room so he made his way to the door.

Chapter 19

The phone jolted her from her sleep and what the call told her had her in a panic. She jumped from her bed, threw on her jogging pants under her nightshirt. She woke up Kayla and told her that she would be back and told her to set the alarm. She pushed her SUV over the limit she was normally comfortable driving.

She arrived at the police station and inquired about him.

"Are you his wife?"

"No, a friend." she told the officer behind the desk.

"Have a seat, I'll see where he is."

She pulled the contents from her purse looking for her phone and couldn't find it. She knew she put her phone in her purse but couldn't find it. She started putting the assortment of things back in when an officer, whose uniform should have been a size bigger stood in front of her.

"Ma'am, his bond hearing is not until the morning."

"What does that mean?"

"That means there is nothing you can do tonight but go home and wait for his hearing tomorrow morning."

"What time?"

"Look, I don't know. You will have to call and find out in the morning." He said as he walked away.

"Excuse me, do you have a phone I can use, I can't seem to find mine?" She asked the officer behind the desk.

"No, look ma'am, just go home, call back at 8 am and someone will be able to tell you something."

He put the magazine back up to his chubby black face. She stood there for another minute and finally walked out. She climbed the stairs as she heard her cell phone ringing. She cursed as she pulled it from the front pocket of her purse. She brushed her finger across the screen and saw Kevin's number

"What do you want?" She yelled into the phone.

"Excuse me?"

"You heard me."

"Oh did your little boyfriend get arrested?" He said with a laugh.

"So you are behind this?"

"Next time he will think twice about coming over here and pulling a gun on me..."

"He did not!"

"Just like you, to stick by his dumb ass."

"Oh, just like I stuck by yours?"

"Where is Kayla?"

"Why?"

"Because I am asking."

"Sleeping."

"Just make sure you have her bring all of her clothes to court tomorrow. I don't want to have to make an extra trip."

She hung up on him as she heard him laughing.

Cheryl tossed and turned all night. When the sun rose, she showered and put on some jeans and a sweater. After changing her clothes four times, she left the house, as Kayla went off to catch the bus. She arrived at the courthouse in La Plata and had to be searched and patted down. She walked into the crowded courtroom and there must have been 200 people in there. The mothers of the 'accused' were all dressed like they were going to church. The "babies' mommas" were dressed like they were going to the club except they had the hollering children with them. The side door opened and in walked all of the men, shackled together. She saw Matthew at the back of the line. He had on the same clothes he had on earlier yesterday. She made eye contact with him and he turned away. One by one each prisoner was called to the defense table, asked if they knew what they were being charged with and then the prosecutor went into his spiel about why the bail should be raised, lowered, or if they should be released or if he should be kept in jail. After two hours Matthew was finally called.

"Matthew Clifton Perry, you are being charged with 1st degree aggravated assault with a deadly weapon, trespassing, and malicious wounding. Do you understand the charges?"

"Yes."

"How do you plead?" the judge asked.

"Not Guilty."

"Mr. Brown, do you have anything you would like to say." The judge asked.

"Well, your honor, due to the nature of this assault, I think Mr. Perry, should at least have his bond set high before trial. You can't just run around beating up the ex-husband of your new girlfriend. Nor can you go around pulling a gun on anyone that makes you mad."

"Your honor, with all due respect, Mr. Perry was merely defending Ms. Bookman. Mr. Goldman continually harasses Ms. Bookman to the point that Mr. Perry went to talk with him and it got out of control."

Kevin jumped up from his seat in the second row, "Out of control! You call him attacking me when I opened my front door, out of control!"

"Order!" The judge shouted, while banging the gavel. "Sir, who are you?"

"I'm Kevin Goldman, the man Mr. Perry attacked."

"Step forward please." The judge ordered.

Kevin stepped up to the prosecutors table. "Your honor, I was in my home and he came to my door and when I opened it, he started punching me." He removed his glasses to show the golf ball sitting under his eye.

"I could have retaliated but I didn't and when I told him to get off of my property, he pulled a gun on me."

The defense attorney spoke, "Your honor. My client has admitted to his part in this assault, but my client has been a victim also."

"Your honor!" the prosecutor yelled.

"Enough! I have enough to make my decision. Mr. Perry, I order that your bond be set at fifty thousand dollars, cash. I also order that you are not to go within 100 feet of Mr. Goldman."

"Your honor." Ms. Tyrell spoke, "Mr. Perry and Mr. Goldman actually do some business together, and that requires that they work closely.

"Not after today." Kevin spoke up.

"Order." The judge snapped while bringing down the gavel again.

"So noted. I suggest that Mr. Perry find another way to do business with Mr. Goldman. Mr. Perry is to stay at least 100 feet away from Mr. Goldman. Ms. Bookman will need to make other arrangements for visitation. Mr. Perry you will be released as soon as you secure bond, trial date will be no less than 60 days from today." She banged her gavel one last time before Kevin shook the hands of his attorney and was led out of the courtroom.

Cheryl looked down at her watch and realized that she needed to make her way to family court. She asked for directions in the lobby and walked towards the offices where the hearings were being held.

One hour after arriving it was ordered that now Kevin and Cheryl shared joint custody of Kayla and that her child support payments would be cut in half. It was also decided that Kayla would spend all holidays with Kevin alternating Christmas and Thanksgiving. Kevin was ordered to go to anger management classes and Cheryl was ordered to take parenting classes.

Cheryl walked out of the courthouse in a daze and tried calling Matthew but he was nowhere to be found. She walked up to her door and saw the note pinned to it.

Hello sweetness, meet me at the gym at 8 for your boxing lessons. See you there.

She went into the house and changed her clothes. She made herself a quick dinner and left Kayla a note that she was meeting Matthew and would be back later. She pulled into the parking lot and there were a few cars but she didn't see Matthew's. She stopped at the desk and asked about the boxing lessons and if Matthew had reserved a room. The woman told her where the gym was located and Cheryl headed off in that direction.

"Oh excuse me." She said as she walked into the first sparring room and saw the man hitting the small bag swinging above his head.

"No problem sweetness." The husky voice replied turning and looking back at her.

The eye patch caught her eye immediately and she backed out of the room. The hair on the back of her arms stood up.

He quickly made his way to her, "Where are you going sweetness?" he said as he pulled her forward and around the corner where the small lockers were located.

"Look, I don't know who you are..." She tried squirming out of his reach, but his fingers dug into her arms harder.

"Matthew is on his way."

He let out a laugh, "aw, poor thing. You actually think that Matthew left that note." He laughed harder this time letting her go. "You really are stupid."

"Cheryl...Cheryl?"

She heard Matthews's voice and so did he.

"Say a word and I will slice him up in front of you." He said as he pulled a knife from out of his glove and opened it with a click. "Now, just walk on out there and don't mention me. Do you understand? Our reunion will be soon enough." He said as he walked around the corner and she heard the other door open and close.

She stood still, her eyes closed trying not to let the tears fall and heard his voice again. She answered him and he came into the room.

"What are you doing here?" he asked her.

"I came to meet you." She said with a half-smile on her face.

"Why?"

"Because I know that you normally workout after a particularly stressful day." She said as she wrapped her arms around him.

He held her close and her body settled into his. He rubbed her back and smoothed her hair. He also noticed the swinging bag in the corner and the unraveled tape and set of boxing gloves on the bench that she stood beside.

He laughed so hard he nearly knocked the pretty young woman down because he didn't notice her. He watched her move away from him and he decided he needed to take the edge off.

As she pushed open the woman's locker room door, he looked around and slipped in behind her before the door closed. He locked the door behind him.

She pulled her sweaty shirt over her head and her long blond hair fell from the clip holding it up. She used her left foot to kick off her right shoe and then kicked off the other. She tugged her shorts down over her slim hips and walked towards the shower.

He moved close to where she was standing and picked up her clothes sniffed them and a smile spread across his face. He heard the shower come on and he moved quickly to the entrance. Her eyes were closed as her fingers raked through her soapy head. Her breasts were tight as her arms were raised. He licked his lips as the water mixed with the suds slid down the crease of her back. He rubbed the front of his pants as he watched her rinse the remaining soap from her hair. He drew in a loud breath and she turned, opening her eyes. He put his finger to his mouth and moved close to her. Her eyes watched as he reached behind her and turned the water off. He grabbed a fistful of her hair and pushed the knife under her neck. He led her to the locker room and made her lay across the bench. He kept the knife in her view as he began unbuttoning his pants.

Matthew led Cheryl upstairs and she fell asleep before he could bring back her water. Her cell phone rang and he found it in her pocket.

"Hello."

"Why did you leave so soon?" said the husky voice.

"Who is this?"

The man continued, "Because you ran out, you made poor Melissa suffer."

"What…who is Melissa?" Matthew asked the caller.

"Shut up! I'm not answering any questions from you. You better keep your eye on her because Kevin is the least of your worries."

The phone went dead.

Chapter 20

Kevin's younger years

"What the fuck are you crying about now?" Henry asked Kevin. "Shut the fuck up! You get on my fucking nerves with all that whining and shit! Get the fuck out of my way. Where is your fucking tramp of a mother?"

"I don't know. She said she would be back and she been gone all day. I didn't have anything to eat after school."

"So what, it'll make a man outta you. Go in that kitchen and fix me a drink. Cognac, straight up and don't make a fucking mess!"

Kevin went into the kitchen and got the bottle down from the cabinet. He poured the drink in Henry's favorite glass and just as he was about to put the bottle back, he heard his mom come through the door.

"Where the fuck have you been!" Henry asked her just before he slapped her across the face.

"Henry, I told you I had to work late at the restaurant. I pulled a double to make extra tips, see." She said holding out the crumpled up money. He snatched it from her and counted it.

"You worked a double and you only made a hundred and fifty dollars. Then you come up in here smelling like another nigga." He started hitting her while she tried ducking. "I'll teach you, you bitch!"

103

He dragged her into the bedroom and Kevin heard him hitting his mother and her begging him not to hit her anymore. Twenty minutes slipped by and he came out sweating and with just his boxer shorts on.

"Where the fuck is my drink?" He yelled into the kitchen.

Kevin took another swig and poured a little more in the glass and took it to him. He snatched it from the ten year old hands, causing it to spill.

"Shit!" He slapped Kevin upside his head. "Go get me another one, and hurry the fuck up!"

Kevin went back into the kitchen when he heard the bedroom door open. He turned and saw his mom walking towards the bathroom. He couldn't take his eyes off of her and when he turned around, he knocked the glass from the counter.

Henry came storming into the kitchen.

"You clumsy bastard, get the hell out of the way." He said while pushing Kevin to the side. He walked into the bathroom and turned on the water. He handed his mom the wet cloth while he held the towel to her bleeding nose. She smiled at him and he smiled back at her.

"Did you eat yet?" She asked him. "I will fix you some macaroni and cheese for dinner and you can go in your room, Ok?" Here take this and don't tell Henry ok?" She whispered as she pulled a couple of twenty's from her bra.

"Why do you let him do that to you?" He whispered as he brushed her hair.

"You're too young to understand. Just don't make him angry, ok?"

Kevin sat the brush down and headed for his room. He put the money in his closet underneath the laundry basket. Henry was sitting in the living room, telling her to hurry up with dinner, while he watched an episode of *Leave It to Beaver*.

His mother made dinner and Henry didn't like it so he threw

it on the floor and she had to clean up the mess.

"See Kevin, this is how you run a house. Let the bitch do all the dirty work."

He started laughing so hard, he blew snot out of his nose. Kevin got out of his chair and started helping his mother clean up the mess.

"Get the fuck up! You aint supposed to be helping her." He said as he snatched the boy up and threw him back into his chair.

"Now hurry up and clean this shit up!" He said as he turned towards Kevin's mother.

After dinner Kevin went to his room. Henry told her that he was going out and she asked when he would be back. The only answer came from the slamming of the door.

The house was quiet when Kevin heard voices in the living room.

"Shh, that bitch might still be up."

"I thought you said you run this house." The voice said.

"I do nigga, I just don't feel like the bull shit tonight."

Kevin left his room and slid along the wall. He looked into the living room and saw the man kneel down in front of Henry. Henry grabbed the back of the guy's head as he moaned.

On his way back to his room he saw his mother, standing in her doorway. She looked at Kevin and closed her door.

Kevin looked down at Rebecca's sleeping form and tried to shake the memory from his head. He ran his hand down her naked body and felt her react. He kissed the back of her neck and she moved over towards him. He needed to release his tension the only way he knew how. He kept stroking her until she woke up and as her eyes opened, he smiled down on her and kissed her neck. He fell back on the pillows after he released himself inside of her and pulled her over onto him. He ran his hands through her tousled hair and kissed her forehead.

"Are you ok?" Kevin asked her.

"Are you serious? I am terrific." Rebecca purred.

"Question…when do you want to start trying to have kids?"

"Are you serious? I am not having any kids." She said as she rose up on her elbows.

"Well we'll see about that." He said as he climbed back on top of her.

"Kevin, I'm serious. I don't want to have any kids." She said as she pushed him off of her. "Besides, I'm already 41 and you are in your 50's, you can't be serious about starting all over, can you?"

"Well yeah. We haven't been using any protection lately. I just assumed it was because you were trying to get pregnant."

"Are you crazy? I take my pills every day." She said as she hopped out of bed and sat on the chair in front of her dresser. "I just got the Atlanta office open and there is no way in hell I am giving that up to start being somebody's momma."

"Well, maybe I need to move up my plans to get someone down there so you can be closer to home. Then maybe you will change your mind."

"Someone down where?" she said as she spun around on the seat.

"In Atlanta, you didn't believe you were going to be there all the time did you?"

"I thought you gave me…"

"Gave you what?" He said starting to laugh.

"The Atlanta office." Rebecca said seriously.

"As in, it's yours. Are you fucking kidding me?" he continued to laugh as he stood up.

"Yes. I'm serious. I thought you said that the Atlanta office is mine." She said as she stood up and followed him in the bathroom.

"No, what I said was, you will be *running* the Atlanta office. I meant for you to oversee the construction, the decorating, hiring the staff and most of all, doing the shit I didn't want to be bothered with."

She folded her arms in front of her.

He was laughing so hard he missed the toilet. "I can't believe you actually thought I was giving that office to you. I guess you have your moments. Look, let's get some sleep. We will talk about it more tomorrow at the office."

He shook, flushed and turned on the water and washed his hands as Rebecca stood in the doorway. He pushed her aside and continued back into the room.

Chapter 21

Cheryl woke up from her nap with Matthew sitting next to her. She smiled up at him and sat up as he stood and sat on the bed.

"What's wrong?"

"I need to ask you something." He said as he rubbed down the left side of his face.

"Ok."

"Was Kevin at the gym today?"

"No, why?"

"Well, I know you went there to meet someone…"

"Correction, I went there to meet you."

"Well, obviously you got the mistaken impression…"

"I wasn't mistaken, there was a note on the door"

"If you say so." He said as he stood his full six foot five frame up and moved across her bedroom."

"Not if I say so…wait…what are you implying? That I lied about meeting you?"

"Well you have lied…"

"Not about this" she shouted.

He held his hands in a defense mode.

She snatched his hands down, "don't give me that. You think I went there to see Kevin?"

"What I know is that you lied about seeing him earlier, you lied about what happened and now you expect me to believe that he wasn't the person at the gym."

"Really Matthew…seriously….I'm not lying about this…it wasn't Kevin." She screamed before storming out of the room.

Matthew followed her down the steps and into the living room where she flopped down on the couch..

"Oh, so you're mad! You're mad? You got some nerve. You are the one who has been lying to me all day and you are mad." His sarcastic tone echoed on the walls of her townhouse.

"I think you better go." She said as she turned on the television.

He yanked the remote from her hands and stood in front of her.

"I need to go? Oh I don't think so. I will not let you get away with that. You might have done that with Kevin, you will not do it with me."

"Do what?"

"Lie."

She blew out a hard breath and rolled her eyes. She folded her arms in front of her and blew out another breath."

"Now, you say it wasn't Kevin, yet you won't tell me who it was. What am I supposed to do? Huh? You tell me…Why can't you understand that I love you more than I love myself? The love I have for you is nothing like I have ever felt in my entire life. You make my day go faster when I know I am going to see you. Shit. I aint a man of many emotions, but you bring them out of me. Cheryl, do you understand I will kill anyone who hurts you. Do you know that? Don't get it twisted, I'm not apologizing for jacking up Kevin, I'm sure it won't be the last time. I said before, I will do anything to protect you and I mean it. Now tell me, what happened after you left the courthouse."

"After you left, I had to go to the juvenile court. Kevin brought me back in for Kayla's custody. They granted him joint custody and she has to spend every other weekend and break with him, starting tomorrow. I got home and there was a note on the door."

"From who?"

"I thought it was from you. You said to meet you at the gym, so I changed…"

"Where is the note?"

She stood and walked into the kitchen and got her purse from the counter, pulled out the crumpled piece of paper and handed it to Matthew.

Chapter 22

Matthew made the decision that they would stay with him for the night until he could figure out what was going on. They walked into his house and Lynette met them at the door

"Would you all like something to eat?" She said as she reached for the overnight bags of Kayla and Cheryl.

"No thank you. Kayla do you want something?" Cheryl asked her daughter.

"No." She answered with attitude. "Can I go to bed now?"

"I'll show her to the guest room." Lynette said.

As she started following Lynette, she turned to Cheryl.

"So I guess just like when Rebecca comes over, you won't have time for me, huh?" she said as she followed behind the older woman.

"Problem?" Matthew asked when Kayla was out of sight.

"She is mad because she and Denise had made plans to go to some teen club in Waldorf, not that she had asked me before making her plans. I honestly don't know what is getting into her lately. Then I told her that she had to go to her dad's house and that didn't go over too well because you know...her friends are over here."

"It's just for the night she should be fine in the morning." He said as he wrapped his arms around Cheryl and her arms circled his waist as she looked up at him. He kissed her lightly at first and then with more hunger. He wanted her but he knew that she might not be as agreeable with her daughter in the house with them.

Cheryl climbed the stairs and found the light in the room Kayla was in, still on. She pushed the door open and saw Kayla sitting on the bed with her phone in her hand.

"Kayla, I think that was very rude. What is the problem with you now?" Cheryl asked while folding her arms.

"Nothing, can you leave, so I can go to bed?" she said as she tossed her phone on the ottoman at the end of the chair, next to the bed. She stood and pulled her sweater over her head.

Cheryl blew out a breath before speaking, "Listen to me young lady, you better get yourself together. You will not talk to me any kind of way, after I am the one giving you everything. Letting you go to your friends' house and have sleepovers with your friends."

"Just so you don't feel guilty about sleeping..."

"You watch your mouth!"

"Get out so I can go to bed!" She screamed as she walked in the bathroom, slamming the door.

Matthew pressed the three switches on the wall and bathed the small room in soft light. He turned the IPod on low and let the smooth jazz fill the air. He sat in the deep brown leather chair closest to the door and smiled at the painting on the wall. Tonight he needed The Special R Cigar by Davidoff. He pulled the cigar from the metal casing and unwrapped it from its clear wrapper. He trimmed the edge and lit it with his engraved lighter. He took a long, satisfying puff from it and let the medium body and the taste of vanilla and butter pull the stress from his body. A knock on the glass door made him open his eyes long enough to see Bo standing there.

"Nigga, don't you ever keep normal business hours?" He

asked while walking into the comfortable space.

"Not when it comes to somebody threatening my family."

Matthew pushed the humidor in Bo's direction and he took out one, lit it and put his massive frame into the chair he had designated as his own.

"Still enjoying the R's, I see." Bo said as he pulled on his cigar.

"Best gift I ever got." Matthew smiled.

"Tell me what you got," He said as his fat hands held firmly onto his cigar. He rolled it until the edges were slightly blackened.

Matthew passed the paper to Bo and they both looked at each other.

"Are you thinking…" Bo started.

"Yes and if this is who I think it is, he just sealed his fate."

"You can't be sure, though." Bo said while holding the cigar in his mouth.

"The handwriting is the same. I thought I had given him enough of a warning last time but I guess he didn't get the message. So now, I guess that message is going to have to be sent much louder."

"Tell me what you want me to do."

Bo finally left after two hours and Matthew headed upstairs. He thought he heard voices so he continued towards the guest bedroom occupied by Cheryl. She was thrashing about the bed and her hands were hitting at the air. He rushed to the bed, trying to grab her hands before she injured herself and her eyes popped open and she fought against him. Not wanting to hurt her, he released her and she sprang from the bed like it was on fire. She held her hands up in a defense stance.

"Please Kevin…I'm sorry." Her voice was low and shaky.

"Cheryl…it's me, Matthew." He said to her.

"Please...please...I'm sorry..."

Matthew approached her slowly and continued calling her name until the glassy look disappeared.

"Matthew?"

"Yes, baby, I'm here."

She threw her arms around him and he pulled her into his arms and picked her up. He laid her down on his bed and climbed in beside her and pulled her close. He smoothed his hand down her unruly hair and whispered that she was safe in his arms and that nothing could harm her.

Chapter 23

Kevin arrived at work after fighting the congestion that was called rush hour and he wasn't sure why it was called that since no one was 'rushing' anywhere. Dropping Corey off at the airport had become much more than a quick trip when all but one lane of the beltway was shut down for an accident. Kevin's mood went further south when he got a ticket for waiting too long in the departure lane at Reagan National. His mood lightened a little when he saw Toni walk in.

She had smoothed her short hair back and had on a red pantsuit, with black four inch heels.

"Good morning." She said while standing in his doorway.

"Good morning. Did you have a good weekend?"

"Definitely. What is planned for today?" she said as she walked over and sat on his desk.

Kevin got up and poured himself a glass of juice. He raised his glass and asked if she wanted a glass. She shook her head no.

She walked up to him and took the glass from his hand, "I'll just have some of yours." She said as she placed the glass near her lips.

"Thank you." She said as she licked her lips and sauntered away.

He smiled as she stopped and winked as she closed the door behind her. He shook his head as he sat down at his desk and swiveled his chair to look out of his eight by four inch window overlooking Lafayette Park

He buzzed her phone, "Toni, can you get Santana on the phone."

"Sure." She said. "Line two sexy."

Before he could respond, he heard Santana's voice on the other end. After asking if he had gotten his agreement in the mail, they started small talk until his other line rang. Placing Santana on hold, he picked up the other line and told the person to hold. He finished up his call with Santana and switched the call to the one he had on hold.

"Yeah, what do you want?" He asked as he picked up line two again.

He slammed the phone down after five minutes and threw the pen at the door just as it opened.

"Is everything ok?" Rebecca asked standing in the doorway.

"Yeah, what do you want?"

"Well good morning to you too. What bee flew into your bonnet?"

"What the fuck is that supposed to mean?"

"Damn, nothing, you are in a mood." she said while folding her arms in front of her.

"Get out of my office. I need to make some phone calls." He said and turned in his chair.

Rebecca turned to leave and then came back and threw the folder on the desk.

Rebecca was fuming as she walked into her office. She didn't like being dismissed by anyone but especially by Kevin.

"Trouble in paradise?" Toni asked as she walked in behind her.

"Mind your business."

"You are my business." Toni said while following Rebecca behind her desk. "You feel tense." Toni said as her hand slid under Rebecca's skirt.

"Toni, stop. We shouldn't be doing this." Rebecca moaned.

"Right." She said as she pulled her hand from under Rebecca's skirt, licked her fingers and walked over and locked the door.

She walked back over to Rebecca and leaned her back onto her desk and dove between her legs.

The handle on the door startled both of them.

"Rebecca?" Kevin said as the door knob turned again.

Rebecca didn't immediately answer but managed to answer him with a weak, "I'm coming."

"Open the door."

"Ok...I'm coming..." Rebecca said, half out of annoyance half out of ecstasy.

Rebecca pushed Toni from between her legs, fixed her skirt and opened the door.

"I need to go out. I'll be back this afternoon."

"Ok, well, I'm going to leave early. I have some things to take care of."

Kevin noticed Toni coming from the bathroom, "Why are you just telling me this."

"Something came up...besides Toni is here."

"She hasn't handled the office by herself yet. Tell you what, why don't everyone take the day off since nobody feels like working today." He said as it was now his turn to storm from someone's office.

"I'll be right back." Rebecca said following after Kevin.

"What the hell is your problem?" She said to him when she walked into the copy room behind him.

"My fucking problem is, nobody came to actually work today! We have a lot of shit to do and now all of a sudden everybody wants a day off!"

"Get off of it Kevin! I came in today after taking care of some of your business and you already had fucking attitude! Let me guess, is it Cheryl this time on one of those spoiled ass kids of yours!"

"Leave it alone Rebecca."

"Oh, leave it alone! Nigga you the one with your ass on your shoulder." She said with a half whisper while looking around to make sure no one could hear their conversation.

"Is there a problem?" Toni asked from behind them.

"No, seems like Kevin is in a mood today. I'm leaving. Make sure you lock up when you leave."

"Look Toni it's been a helluva day. Set the alarm when you leave and we will start fresh tomorrow."

Kevin walked into the bed and breakfast and was greeted by the teenager behind the counter.

"Can I help you?" She said with a twist of her hair in her fingers.

"Yeah, is Cheryl here?"

"May I tell her whose asking?"

"No. Is she in back?" He asked while walking behind the counter.

"Umm, sir, she is in a mee…" she said while he pushed by her.

The door slammed open and Matthew stepped away from her.

Cheryl spoke up, "It's ok Destiny. What do you need Kevin?"

"I need to talk to you in private." He said while he sat down in the chair in front of her desk.

"Not going to happen." Matthew spoke up.

"Nigga, this ain't got shit…"

Cheryl stepped in between both men.

"Wait a minute. First of all this is my office. What do we need to talk about? Matthew, can you give us a few minutes?"

"I'll be right outside." Matthew said while giving her a kiss.

"Nigga, ain't nobody going to do nothing to this bi…"

The door shut and Kevin watched her walk behind her desk.

"Donnell called."

"I know."

"Should have known his bitch ass would be running under your skirt, or should I say wearing it."

"If you came here to insult my child."

"Oh, your child?"

"Yes, you are the one who said you didn't want him calling you."

"So what the fuck he calling me for then?"

"Lower your voice." Cheryl said as she looked towards the door.

"Don't tell me what the fuck to do!" He said while standing.

"Cheryl. You ok?" Matthew said, while pushing the door further open.

"Yes, I'm ok. Can you close the door?" Cheryl continued, "Donnell told me that you didn't finish paying his last semester yet."

"I told his bitch ass that I would."

"Why do you have to always call people names?"

"Whatever. That nigga had the nerve to give me a fucking deadline."

"Kevin, he needs it paid so that he can get his cap and gown for graduation."

"A graduation that his faggot ass didn't invite me too."

Cheryl stood, "ok, obviously it's not in you to speak like an adult."

"So you're saying I am good enough to pay his fucking tuition but not good enough to get a fucking invitation?"

"Would you have gone?" She asked him, walking past his chair.

"I don't know, but he never gave me the fucking option."

"Well, I told him that he shouldn't waste the invitation if you weren't going to come."

"I should have known your crazy ass would tell him some shit like that. Well, maybe since I don't get an invite, maybe I might forget to pay the balance."

"You would be that spiteful?" she said, pouring herself a glass of water.

"Don't tell me about being spiteful. You're the bitch who told him not to the send the fucking invitation!"

"Because you are the one acting like you don't know him. You have barely acknowledged him since he came out about being gay. You treat him like he has a disease or contagious, so why should he invite you?"

"Because I'm that nigga's father."

"Only when you want to be." She said as she walked back towards her desk.

"What the fuck is that supposed to mean?" he said blocking her path.

She stopped in front of him, "Besides, they say being gay is not a choice, but maybe it's hereditary."

He grabbed her and the glass dropped from her hand. She gasped as he pulled her close to him, his hand in a fist.

Matthew rushed through the door and pulled Kevin around to him.

The fight was on as the two men began yelling and punching. Kevin fell to the floor with Matthew on top of him and Cheryl tried pulling them apart.

"Stop it! You're gonna hurt him!" She yelled. "Stop it! Matthew, stop it! Good lord, please stop Matthew you are hurting him!" she said finally prying him off of her ex-husband.

Kevin was in a heap on the floor. Blood was pouring from his nose and his eye was swollen shut. His lip looked like it had been split into four sections.

"Matthew what did you do? What have you done?" She said as she kneeled down over Kevin.

"You have got some nerve." He said breathing hard. "You are gonna protect that nigga. Are you fucking serious Cheryl? That nigga had his fucking hands around you throat!"

Cheryl stood, "Matthew just go. I'll come by later."

"Don't fucking bother." He said and stormed out, slamming the door.

Kevin stood, spit out blood on her carpet. "Get the fuck out of my way!" He said and walked out of the door with Cheryl behind him.

"Destiny, please call the carpet cleaners and have them clean this before morning. I am leaving for the day."

"Are you ok?" Destiny asked.

"I'll be fine. If Matthew calls, tell him I'm on my way."

She drove towards Waldorf, and stopped along the way to pick up some yellow roses. She then stopped in the food court at the Hawaiian Grill and got some of his favorite chicken. She arrived at his development, but the gates were closed. She entered the code and the gate opened. She parked behind his silver Mercedes and Lynette opened the door and told her he was downstairs in the gym. She heard him grunting and the weights clanging down as he did his repetitions.

"Hey." She said nervously.

"What do you want?" He said without looking at her.

"I got you something." She said as she pushed the flowers toward him.

"I can smell them." He said.

"You aren't going to look."

"Who are those for? Kevin?"

"Matthew don't." She said as she walked closer to him "I'm trying to apologize."

"For what?"

"What?" she asked.

"You aren't deaf. What are you apologizing for?" He said as she sat up and stared at her hard.

Her breath caught as she looked at him and then away from him, "For...umm..."

"Go back to Kevin." He said as he leaned back and picked the weights up again.

"You're not being fair." She said, while kneeling down in front of him. He stopped lifting the weights and sat up.

"You want to talk to me about being fair? How about this for fair, when I run in your office and he has his hands around your fucking neck. How about this for fair? When I defend you, you run to him and cradle him in your arms. How about this for fair? You look at him like you still love him. You tell me what's fair."

"Matthew, you have it all wrong. I was only trying to protect you."

"How were you protecting me?" He said as he got up and brushed around her on his way to the punching bag hanging in the corner.

"You were going to kill him. I could see it in your eyes."

"Death is too good for him."

"Don't say that!"

"There you go again, protecting him."

"I am not!" She said to his back.

"When it comes to the people I love, nothing matters to me. So if I kill him, oh well."

"What the hell!" she started walking away but doubled back. "You are pathetic. How did I ever think I was in love with you? You are just as crazy as Kevin!" She walked off but Matthew caught her by the arm.

"Really? You think I'm as crazy as him! Maybe I need to be! Maybe I need to treat you like he treats you!" He said, pushing her backwards.

"Stop it!"

"No, maybe I need to treat you like you are used to being treated!"

"Matthew, stop it!" She said, her hands slapping at his sweating arms.

He kept pushing her until she was against the mirrored wall.

"Stop it!" She put her hand on his sweaty chest. He slapped it away.

"No, this is what you want? Right?" He said.

"Stop it Matthew, please stop it. Matthew stop..." His lips crushed hers and he pushed his tongue into her mouth.

"I'm not going to stop until I'm done." Matthew growled in her ear.

In one quick motion, they were on the floor, with him on top of her and tearing away her pants, he used his feet to pull his pants down. His face was contorted with anger. He pushed himself into her.

"Matthew. Please." she said again and this time he stared down at her and then rolled off of her.

"Shit...shit!" he yelled as Cheryl took deep breaths and the tears rolled down the side of her face. "Cheryl....I'm....shit!" he got up and grabbed his shorts from the floor. Cheryl got up, following him into the bathroom.

He stood in front of the sink, hands resting on the counter and his breaths were ragged as if he couldn't get enough air in his lungs.

She said his name softly and touched his shoulder. He turned and looked at her, caressed her face and wrapped his arms around her so tightly it sucked the air from her momentarily.

"I love you." He said.

"I love you too." she said as they began kissing each other. She pushed the door closed and for the next few minutes, nothing mattered in that small space. Their moans filled the air until they could not hold back and they both climaxed.

They showered and she told Matthew that she would return later. She would take Kayla to Kevin's house and she promised him that they would have a nice quiet evening.

Chapter 24

Kevin entered his house, poured himself and drink and was stopping his nose from bleeding when his phone rang.

"What the fuck do you want?" he said into the phone. "Just bring her whenever you want." he said as he slammed the phone down.

He sat down in the office and tried going over the numbers for the Atlanta office, but his massive headache wouldn't let him do anything but put his head on his desk and close his eyes.

He opened his eyes and had to adjust to the darkness. His cell phone was vibrating, at the same time the doorbell was ringing. He brushed the empty Jack Daniels bottle off of the desk and into the trashcan.

Kevin opened the door and his daughter brushed past him without a word.

Cheryl walked in behind her as Kevin stepped aside. She walked into the kitchen and grabbed a dish towel and put ice in it and held it out to him. He snatched it from her hand and put it on his mouth.

"I think you might need a couple of stitches. Do you want me...?" she said.

"I don't need you to do shit for me!"

"Kevin, I'm trying to help you." she said, sucking in a deep breath.

"Bullshit! You don't care about me, you are only concerned about that nigga of yours and your faggot son!"

"Forget it! I'm leaving!" she said as she slammed the ice tray on the counter.

"Good. I didn't invite you in anyway."

Before leaving she turned to him, "You need to make sure that you keep ice on it for at least a couple of hours. The swelling will go down, then you need to massage it every couple of minutes, so that it doesn't get black and blue. But don't feel pressured to take my advice." As she opened the door, she heard him say thanks.

"Look, let me look at it again before I leave." She turned and walked back towards the living room. "You might not need stitches, and don't eat anything with salt on it, cause it's going to burn like hell. You really should get out of those pants. I could probably get the blood out if you want."

"Without taking them to the cleaners?"

"There are a few tricks I learned while *only* being a football mom. Remember, Donnell always had a bloody mouth or nose and there was never a blood stain on his yellow jersey. I know my way around a laundry room."

She walked away from him, when he got too close to her and quickly sidestepped him, knowing full well that it was the alcohol making him be civil for the moment.

"Go upstairs and change. I'll start the washer."

Kevin came down in just his briefs and handed her the pants. Kevin was standing close enough to her that she could smell the Michael Jordan cologne he was wearing. As she turned to leave, he stepped closer to her and wrapped his arms around her. Her breathing quickened because she knew that now was the time she needed to exit quickly before things got out of hand.

"I'm not going to hurt you." He said into her ear. He pressed himself into her.

"Kevin...don't."

"You know you want me." He slurred.

"Kevin, I am only here to help you..."

He started kissing her neck. His hands came up to her breasts and squeezed.

"Kevin, don't do this." She said while trying to push him away from her. He grabbed her hands.

"Don't fight me."

"Kevin please don't do..." she whispered, trying not to cry.

"This is what you came here for isn't it." He said into her ear.

"No...no I didn't." she whispered.

He used his foot to shut the door to the laundry room. He released her hands and she tried getting around him. He pushed her back against the dryer and pushed his hands down her pants. He unbuttoned her pants, pulling them down in the process and slid his fingers inside of her. He used his other hand to pull his briefs down. She struggled but his hand came up to her neck and prevented the words of protest from exiting her mouth.

When he was done, he released her arms and pulled up his briefs. He opened the door and walked through the kitchen and into his office. She pulled her pants up and walked into the bathroom to clean herself up. When she was done, she walked through the kitchen and out the front door.

Kevin heard the front door open and close. He poured himself another drink and gulped it down while sitting down at his desk and turned on the computer. He answered a few emails and sent a few.

He logged into his favorite website and smiled when he saw his favorite girl was logged on.

Kissmehard: hey sexy. I almost logged off. I didn't think you

127

were logging on.

Suxcesblkman: I had a few things to take care of. You know I couldn't miss talking to you.

Kissmehard: LOL. Yeah right.

Suxcesblkman: well, kinda

Kissmehard: how was your day?

Suxcesblkman: hard as hell

Kissmehard: what happened?

Suxcesblkman: the bitch of an ex-wife of mine and her new boyfriend set me up

Kissmehard: how

Suxcesblkman: she told my faggot son not to send me an invite to his graduation but that nigga had the nerve to call me and ask for money

Kissmehard: how many times do I have to tell you not to use that word?

Suxcesblkman: what word

Kissmehard: faggot

Suxcesblkman: oh, sorry, forgot you were SENSITIVE

Kissmehard: look, just don't use it.

Suxcesblkman: n e way, I went to ask her about it and her dumb ass told him not to send me one. See that's why she was always getting her fucking ass kicked because she always did dumb shit!

Kissmehard: is this why you logged on. I ain't trying to hear all of this, now tell me what I want to hear.

Suxcesblkman: oh, about how I want to fuck you when we finally meet.

Kissmehard: yes and what else

Suxcesblkman: and how I want you to take me in your mouth and suck me until I go limp

Kissmehard: Mmmm and how I am gonna make you fuck my ass until I beg you to stop

Suxcesblkman: but I'm not going to stop. Then I'm gonna go down on you and have you squirming under me while I finger your ass with my tongue in your pussy.

Kissmehard: I'm getting wet just thinking about it.

Suxcesblkman: when am I gonna meet you. It's been almost a year and every time you set up a meeting place something happens. I can't wait much longer.

Kissmehard: well, just imagine when it does happen, it will be explosive

Suxcesblkman: or something.

Kissmehard: Does your fiancé know that I am you online wife

Suxcesblkman: hell no! And she won't. Unless you tell her, but you know what will happen if you do.

Kissmehard: yes, no more money.

Suxcesblkman: that's right. Now open wide, because I have been waiting to give you something

Kissmehard: is it creamy

Suxcesblkman: yep

Kissmehard: white

Suxcesblkman: yep

Kissmehard: give it to me poppie

Suxcesblkman: shit. I'm about to cum

Kissmehard: I'm ready

Suxcesblkman: ugh….Mmm….ugh….shit. I have messed up my damn pants

Kissmehard: oh…you naughty boy, do you need a spanking.

Suxcesblkman: yes, that's what I need.

Kissmehard: bend over poppie

Suxcesblkman: Mmmm

Kissmehard: do you feel my tongue on your ass.

Kissmehard: Poppie?

Kissmehard: You still here?

Kevin logged off, went back to his bar and poured himself a drink. She had broken the rules. He sat back in his chair and his mind drifted back to his childhood.

From that point on, Henry paid Kevin a visit twice a week for almost four years. Each time he came into his room, it was when his mom was "entertaining" Henry's friends.

"Look, tonight we are doing something different." Henry whispered when he entered the boy's room.

"I don't feel good." Kevin whined.

"Stop being a baby." He said while pulling his boxer's down. "Now listen I want you to lie on your stomach. I'm going to show you how real sex feels." He said while he laid his foul-smelling body on the boy. He pushed his penis deep into his young body and Kevin started screaming but Henry pushed the boy's head into the pillow.

When Kevin woke up, Henry was gone and Kevin was lying in a puddle of his own urine. When he wouldn't come out of his room the next day, his mother came and sat on the bed and stroked his forehead.

"Are you ok?"

"I don't want him here anymore." he said to his mother.

"Honey, he makes more money than me so he has to be here for a little while longer...I thought you liked Henry."

"I hate him!" Kevin said while jumping up from the bed.

"Hate is such a strong word. You might not like him, but you don't hate him."

"Yes I do! I hope he dies!" he said as he went into the bathroom. His mother announced she was heading to work through his door. Ten minutes after his mother left, Henry was standing in his doorway.

"So you hate me?" He said with a laugh. "As long as you do

what I tell you to do, I don't care if you hate me. I ain't your fucking friend, you got that?"

Kevin stared at him and Henry walked to the bed, yanked him up and punched him in the face.

"Don't you ever eye me boy!"

Kevin's punishment was that he had to perform oral sex on Henry and then let him use his young body as a toilet.

Kayla's voice shook him from the memory as he heard her yelling about her computer not working.

"What the fuck do you want me to do about it?" he yelled back.

"Never mind!" she said as she slammed the door to her bedroom. He walked up the stairs and heard her talking to someone.

"He gets on my damn nerves. No girl. He is always acting all shitty when I ask him something. That's why I hate coming over here. No girl, when I got picked up for violating curfew, my dad took my mom back to court so now I'm being punished and being made to come over here every other week." Kayla laughed.

He slammed her door open, "Oh, so I get on your nerves? I don't get on your nerves when I'm buying you shit do I? Do I get on your nerves when I'm paying your fucking cell phone bill every fucking month? Do I get on your nerves when I'm handing you my fucking credit card so you can buy those fucking Apple Bottom jeans your ass is wearing?" he snatched her up from the bed.

"I'm calling mom!" She said while trying to get past him. He grabbed her arm and swung her back into the wall.

"Who the fuck do you think you are?" He yelled in her face.

"Why you listening to my phone conversations!"

"This is my house young lady and I can listen to whatever the fuck I want to!"

"You get on my nerves!"

"You ungrateful little brat! You and your fucking mother are just alike!" he yelled while grabbing her arm.

"Get off of me!" She said while trying to free herself from his grip.

Kevin slapped her over and over. When he was finished her nose was bleeding and she had swelling under her eye.

"Shut the fuck up! You better not let me hear that shit again! Do you understand me?" He said yanking her door open and slamming it closed.

Kayla grabbed her phone from the floor and started texting.

Chapter 25

Cheryl arrived home and quickly showered. Her phone started to vibrate on the nightstand.

Call from 3526867

She ignored it and it immediately started to vibrate again.

Call from 5491823

She walked downstairs and went into the kitchen and got the bottle of Linganore Sparkling Red Wine from the refrigerator. She grabbed a glass from the cabinet and walked into the living room. Instead of drinking the wine, she saw the bottle of Sveka Vodka on the sofa table and decided to drink that. After two glasses of vodka and ruby red grapefruit juice, she heard the phone in the distance, but was a little too tipsy to get up to answer it.

She heard her front door open and then heard his voice.

"Cheryl? Are you here?" Matthew said.

"Yes." She slurred.

He let out a laugh, "What in the hell? Are you drunk?"

"No." She said while standing and swaying.

Matthew carried her to bed and her phone vibrated again.

Meet me in an hour the text said.

He wasn't sure he should answer her text but his gut was telling him something wasn't right. He typed in a response and waited. The answer came and his stomach tightened.

He kissed Cheryl on the cheek and ran down her stairs. He made sure to set her alarm and when he reached his car he called his friend Bo. He then called his ex-wife and told her not to go anywhere and to make sure Tamia stayed home. Tonight would be the night that he dealt with his past, once and for all.

Kevin finished the bottle of cognac and was about to turn in when his doorbell rang. He opened it and was hit by a wild punch that knocked the wind out of him momentarily.

"I told you! I told you not to put your hands on my sister!" Donnell spit out as his hands connected once again.

Kevin regained his composure, and within seconds had his son pinned to the floor.

Kevin fought as hard as he could until he was pulled from his son and now had to defend himself against not only his son but his son's lover. The red and blue flashing lights momentarily blinded him as he was being pulled from the floor and his hands twisted behind his back. Kayla stood screaming and crying but her words were clear. She was accusing her father of starting the entire incident and he was being arrested.

The officer asked him if he knew the two victims.

"Victims? They are not victims. I live here, this is my goddamn house and they came in here like they lived here. I have the right to defend my property."

"Sir, you didn't answer the question. Do you ..."

"That's my son." He said as Donnell and Kayla walked out supporting each other.

"Oh, can you tell me what happened?"

"I don't know. I opened my door and all of a sudden his faggot ass was swinging. I defended myself against him...Look I want to press charges."

The officer turned him around and released his hands, "Are you sure?"

"Are you kidding me?"

"Well, do you want to give your statement now, or would you like to do it after you take a ride to the emergency room?"

"What will happen to him?"

"He will be in custody until you give your statement."

"Good. I'll go to the emergency room first and then I'll be down afterwards.

He watched as they handcuffed his son and his lover. His daughter was told to go into the house by the female officer and she walked past him in a huff, slamming the door behind her. He went in behind her, ran up the stairs to her room and slapped her once across the face.

"You ungrateful bitch! Just like your mother, get your shit because I am calling you a fucking cab so you can get the hell out of my house!" he shouted as he walked to his bedroom, called the cab and went to the den to wait. The cab blew its horn about twenty minutes later and he yelled for her to get down there. He walked out, gave the cabbie the address and the money. She stormed past him and slammed the door as she got into the black cab.

He walked back inside and his hand was now throbbing. His eye was swollen shut and his breathing was becoming more of an effort than it should have been. He decided to go to the emergency room where they promptly told him that he had two broken ribs and a bruised lung, which would require him staying overnight for observation.

After telling the third doctor, for about the fifth time, what happened, they finally got him settled in his room. He called Rebecca and left a message for her to come down to the hospital.

Chapter 26

Arriving at Toni's townhouse, Rebecca used her key to enter the nicely decorated space. She was impressed by how quickly Toni had set up her home. Toni was sitting in the living room with a glass of wine and the television remote in her hand.

Rebecca leaned over the couch and kissed her on the cheek. "Did you lock up everything and put the alarm on?" she asked as she walked around the couch, took the glass from Toni's hand and drank from it.

"I'm not an amateur, I know how to lock up an office Rebecca." she said, taking her glass back. "Are you going to stand there all night or are you going to join me?" she said.

Rebecca sat down next to Toni, curling her legs up under herself.

"What are you watching?"

"Turn it on and see for yourself." She said handing her the remote.

After a few minutes of watching the television, Toni whispered in her ear, "Do you like seeing me with someone else?"

"Who is he?"

"His name is not important but he had some serious skills."

Toni touched Rebecca's face, turning it toward her and kissed her lightly on the mouth. Rebecca's hands pulled her closer to her and she moaned as Toni's teeth found that space on her neck that drove her wild. For the next hour, the video watched them as they writhed around on the sofa until they couldn't contain themselves and they collapsed in a heap against the pillows.

Rebecca got up first, walking towards the bathroom as Toni walked towards the kitchen. She heard her cellphone vibrate again and walked over and picked it up.

She started throwing on clothes when Toni came from the bathroom

"What's wrong?"

"Kevin is at the hospital." She scanned the room, found the rest of her clothes, and quickly dressed and headed to the hospital.

"I'll go with you." She announced.

"I don't think that would be wise."

"And why not?"

"Look, I already missed his call and now I am not even sure if he is still there."

"Calm down. Call while I drive." Toni said as she slid her feet into the mules by the couch and grabbed her jacket from the chair by the door.

After a few minutes on the phone with Rebecca being transferring back and forth between the emergency room receptionist and the front desk, they finally learned that Kevin had been admitted. They arrived and Toni parked.

They rushed in and Rebecca went to the desk. "I'm looking for Kevin Goldman."

"Was he brought here?"

"Why do you think I'm asking for him?" Rebecca said with an attitude.

The woman looked down and mumbled something as she started tapping the computer keys. She finally looked up and told them that he was in room 2980 East.

They walked in and saw him hooked up to an IV with an oxygen tube running to his nose. One eye was the size of a golf ball and was an ugly shade of purple. The covers were around his waist and he had tape around his middle section. He had a cast one his right hand and stitches on his bottom lip.

"Hey you." Rebecca whispered. "What happened?"

His eyes fluttered open. "Hey sexy. You got here quick."

"I got here as quick as I could. What happened?

"Kayla called her brother after I had to get on her ass about her mouth. He came over to the house and bum rushed me."

"Oh my God! Donnell?" She said with a hand to her mouth.

"That fucking faggot thought he was getting money from me, he ain't got shit coming from me but a police report, and that bitch ass daughter of mine, I don't want to see her fucking ass again."

"Kevin, what are you saying? You don't mean that."

"Like hell I don't. Do you see what they did to me?"

"I'd hate to see what you did to them."

"What the fuck is that supposed to mean?"

"Nothing, look just rest. You have had one helluva day." She said as she turned towards Toni. "You better go."

Chapter 27

Matthew wondered why now? Why had Galen picked now to come back into his life? He took his mother away from him and he was lucky that Matthew didn't kill him that night in the alley. He could have beat him to death with his bare hands, but someone thought his sorry ass was worth saving and called the cops. Matthew had lived with his moment of weakness for far too long but tonight he was not going to have any such moment. Tonight would be the night that he finished off what he had started five years ago. His thoughts were interrupted by a woman's voice behind him.

"Matt? Matthew Perry is that you? What you doing hanging out in that building. Now you do know what goes on around here after dark. You better get on over here and give your auntie some suga."

Matthew walked quickly over to the only person that helped him five years ago. She was the only person that knew his pain.

"Uh, hey Miss Houston. How are you doing? What are you doing out at this time of night?"

"Chile couldn't sleep. I feel a little antsy, and whenever I get that feeling, something bad is gonna happen."

"Well, I wouldn't worry about it." He said while walking her towards her building.

"Well, you be careful." She said as she stepped up on her stoop. Don't go getting yourself into any trouble down here. You

139

hear me? Let sleeping dogs lie. You go on home now. You hear?" She said as she walked into the door and let it close behind her.

He watched as she continued down the hallway to her first floor apartment. He was lost in thought when the first blow hit him. He felt himself falling forward and before he could regain his composure, something hit the back of his leg that sent him sprawling towards the concrete sidewalk.

He rolled away and grabbed the attacker's ankle and pulled him down. He heard the body hit the pavement beside him and he had opened his pocket knife before falling. He drove the knife into the person's leg and they let out a howl that would wake the dead. He felt another swing barely miss his head but he felt the air blow by his ear. He was just about to get up when he felt something hard against the side of his face and heard a pop. The immediate jolt of pain sent Matthew crashing back down to the concrete. He drew his gun and just as he was about to fire, he heard Mrs. Houston's voice saying she had called the police. He heard the feet scrambling and heard them running away from the alley. He got up and leaned against the dumpster and ducked inside of the abandoned building. The police drove by with the search light pointed down the alleyway.

He walked into his house with a massive headache and a huge lump on the side of his face. He tried to get past Lynette's door before she woke up but it was too late. She didn't say a word as she came out of her room, passing him in the hallway. He got to his room and laid back on his bed. His door opened and she walked in with a bag of ice and a disapproving look.

"First of all, it's none of my business what you went out here and did. All I know is I have only seen that look one other time before. I don't want to know what happened, all I want to know is, is the other guy still living?" She said while handing him the ice.

"For the time being." He answered her without looking up.

"What does that mean?" She said with her hands on her wide hips.

"His best bet would be to stay in hiding because if I find him or his contacts."

Realization hit him and he jumped up and shouted that he needed to check on something while running past Lynette on his way out the door.

He drove to his ex-wife's house and banged on her door until she snatched it open.

"What!" She said while blocking his path into the house and pulling her robe closed.

"Are you and Tamia ok?"

"Why?"

"Just answer the fucking question." He shouted as he walked towards the back.

"Nigga, why you here looking busted up. What, you and your new girls ex get into it?" She laughed.

"I can see you are as spiteful as ever." He said as he turned and looked at her.

"Well, if you can see that, than you can see I'm ok. Tamia is at a friend's house and I have company. Good night." she said as she held the door open and watched him walk out of it.

She walked back towards her bedroom with a smile on her face. Galen was still butt naked in her bed, awaiting her return. She dropped her robe and climbed onto her bed. He pulled her down to him and kissed her much rougher than he had before.

"Whoa, why you being so rough?" she asked as she pushed away from him.

"Look, c'mon. You took long enough that I aint even in the mood anymore."

141

"Well, then maybe you need to bounce." She said as she rolled completely away from him.

"Oh hell no, I came here for one thing.."

She cut him off, "well, now I aint in the mood. Get on!" she said with a wave of her hand.

"Bitch! Who do you think you are talking to?" he said as he grabbed her by the hair and snatched her off of the bed.

"Get your damn hands off of me!" she yelled while slapping his hands away.

Before she said another word, she was falling into a heap on the floor with him standing over her.

Chapter 28

As he pulled up into Cheryl's driveway he saw a tan colored Mercedes in the driveway. He pulled in behind the Mercedes and saw a woman who was a cross between Toni Braxton and Halle Berry, sitting in the passenger seat. Rebecca was standing at the door talking to Cheryl.

"Look, now that you have delivered the news, you can go." He heard Cheryl say as he walked up. He kissed her on the cheek and took the spot next to her.

"What you need to do is tell your son and his *girlfriend* to apologize for what they did to Kevin."

"You've got some nerve." Cheryl said, "I will not tell him such a thing. Maybe instead of defending him, you might want to see what he did to Kayla."

"I don't care..." Rebecca started to say.

"Well, that doesn't surprise me. I'll tell you this, you better be careful, or you will be next. Good night." she said as she let Matthew by and shut the door."

"What happened?" Matthew started to say.

"Maybe I should be asking you that." She said while looking at the increasingly growing lump on the side of his head and the blood on his clothes.

"I asked you first." He said

"Kayla came home in a cab after Kevin hit her in the mouth and apparently him and Donnell got into a fight and...well it's just too much." Cheryl said. "So are you going to tell me?" she said while looking at him.

"Look, I had a little situation that I had to handle…"

"With Kevin?"

"No, look we will talk about it in the morning. It's been one hell of a night." he said as he walked to the stairs.

"Are you ok?" Galen asked Sherrie

"Get the hell out of my house! Ain't no nigga ever put their fucking hands on me, and you are just a nigga I fuck occasional…you damn sure ain't going to be doing it!"

"Look it was an accident."

"I said get the fuck out. I don't want to hear it! If you don't leave right now, I'm calling the cops."

Galen grabbed his shirt from the floor and stepped over her, hitting her in the shoulder with his foot.

Sherrie got up and went into the bathroom and saw the bruise and swollen eye. She wasn't prepared to tell Matthew what happened. She stepped into the shower and washed all traces of the man she knew as Malcolm away from her. She knew she should have pressed harder when she saw his driver's license had a different name but figured it wasn't the time to do it when she woke up on the floor.

Chapter 29

Cheryl hadn't heard from Kevin, Kayla was barely talking to her and Matthew wouldn't give her a straight answer as to what had happened to him a few nights ago. Her bed and breakfast was busier than usual. Summer was coming and people were either booking for their honeymoon or for a quick summer getaway.

Walking in, she saw her employee behind the counter and asked her if she had any calls. When Brittany told her that her husband had called, Cheryl quickly reminded her that he was her ex-husband and asked what he wanted.

"I am not sure. He said to call him at the hospital. He left his room number."

She quickly took the message and went into her office and shut the door. She called the hospital and was put through to his room.

"Hello."

"Uh, hi. Is this Kevin Goldman's room?"

"Yes."

"Can I speak with him?"

"Who's calling?" the woman asked.

"Cheryl."

"Yeah."

"Kevin. What is wrong? Why are you in the hospital?" she said into the phone.

145

"Don't act new. You knew damn well I was here."

"No I didn't. Is this from when you and Matthew…"

"It would take more than his dumb ass to put me here."

"I'm on my way." She said as she dropped the phone into the receiver and grabbed her purse on the way out of the door. She told Brittany that she would return later.

On her way to the elevators, she saw Rebecca holding hands with another woman. She pushed the button to head up to the second floor.

"Kevin. What happened?" she said as she walked into his room.

"Good afternoon. Are you Mrs. Goldman?" the nurse said as she finished wrapping the bandage around his mid-section.

Kevin and Cheryl answered simultaneously, "No."

"I used to be." Cheryl answered.

"I traded up." He said with a roll of his eyes.

The nurse exchanged dirty looks with Kevin before turning her attention to Cheryl.

"Well. I was just telling Mr. Goldman that he needed to stay a couple more days because his ribs are healing nicely, but his lung still has us concerned."

"His lung?"

"Yes, the bruise he has is taking a little longer to heal and we really need to monitor him closely in case his lung collapses. We are hoping it doesn't happen but if it does we would rather for him to already be here in the hospital."

"Like I told you before, if it hasn't happened yet, it won't." Kevin said while sitting up.

Cheryl spoke up, "But it could happen. Why not just stay here for one more day…"

"I really don't need you telling me shit!"

"I'll leave you two alone and I'll be back to check on you in another hour, then we can decide."

146

"Kevin, why do you always have to be so mean? It's for your own good, unless you want to be back in here longer if your lung collapses."

"Look, why the fuck are you here? I don't recall asking you to come here. If this is about Kayla's swollen lip, it will heal."

Another nurse walked in, "Don't go upsetting my patient, you hear." She said as she gave Kevin a wink.

"It's ok Theresa it's just my ex-wife."

"Look I don't care who it is, she better not upset you. You need your rest." She said leaving as she pulled the door closed behind her.

"I swear, you think you would learn." She said as she put her purse down and walked to the window.

"What the fuck did you say?" He said.

"Kevin, why would you hit her like that? You better be glad…"

"What? That bitch should be glad all I did was hit her in the mouth."

"Then how did you end up here." She asked while folding her arms across her chest.

"I was wondering when your dumb ass was going to ask me that. Kayla called Donnell…what the hell are you smiling about?" He said as he sat up in his bed.

"I'm not smiling." she started to say.

"I will get the last laugh on his faggot ass. He is in jail because I pressed charges against him. Let's see how he finishes school with a felony on his record."

"You're serious? You had my son arrested…and you're pressing charges. After all I have done for you, you are going to press charges against my son?"

"You damn right! And what does that supposed to mean, all you have done for me?"

"I mean, I never pressed charges against you…"

147

"I didn't tell you not too." He said as he leaned back.

"Really, you have nerve." She said while walking towards his bed. "All of the times you hit me, I never once called the police on you and now because Donnell hit you a couple…"

"What the fuck did you just say to me? You better be glad I'm still hooked up to this fucking IV or this bed would become yours."

"I'm just saying that because Donnell got a couple of good shots in on you, now you want to ruin his chance of graduating, just because you are what…um, embarrassed. That seems about right. Is that it, you are embarrassed that your gay son kicked your ass, seems like it is poetic justice if you ask me. He used to watch you beat me all the time so I guess you actually taught him a few things. Ha, Ha, Ha, it's sad really. Tell you what, I'll pay for his school my damn self."

"Good, and while you're at it, start paying for Kayla's private school. That bitch aint getting another dime out of me!"

"Oh no you don't! It's in the divorce that you will pay for it, don't make me take you to court."

"Get the fuck out of my room!"

"Ma'am, I'm going to have to ask you to leave." The nurse announced.

"Gladly." Cheryl said while snatching up her purse.

"Don't fucking come back either!" He yelled to her back.

Chapter 30

She picked up her keys, left Kayla a note and drove to the only place she knew people would understand.

The receptionist gave her the clipboard with the forms and after answering the easy ones, the harder ones became more difficult to answer.

"Mrs. Goldman?" She said.

"Yes."

"I'm glad you came back." She said with a smile.

She returned her smile and completed the questionnaire and went to the desk to give it back to the receptionist.

Linda came through the door again and asked Cheryl to follow her. She led Cheryl into a small corner office, barely big enough to hold her desk and chair, however she had a file cabinet situated behind the door, a chair behind her desk and a small microwave beside the extra chair.

Linda sat down and took a sip from her coffee mug, "What made you come in today?"

"Well, I... I decided that I needed to make changes."

"Does your husband know you are here?"

"No. Actually we aren't married anymore."

"Good for you."

"I guess." She answered.

"Why do you sound so unsure?"

"Because the divorce has been final for almost three years,

and he still has issues."

"What kind of issues?"

"He still puts me down."

"Does he still hit you?"

"Not really."

"The answer to that would be a yes or no."

"I guess."

"Mrs. Gold...I'm sorry, what is your name now."

"Ms. Bookman."

"Ms. Bookman, can you look at me, in the eye, and give me a yes or no answer. Does Mr. Goldman still hit you?"

After a few seconds, she finally answered.

"Yes."

"So, why does he still hit you?"

"I guess I make him mad."

"By doing what?"

"Well, Kayla, that's our daughter, got picked up by the police and I should have known where she was."

"Did she tell you where she was going?"

"Yes."

"So, she didn't go there."

"Yes she did, but she also went somewhere else and was in DC past curfew."

"Did you know she was in DC?"

"No. I would never have let her go."

"So tell me again, why he hit you. You just told me you knew she was supposed to be one place, but obviously she went somewhere else, didn't tell you nor did she tell him, and he hit you because...."

"Because I should have known."

"Did he know?"

"No."

"When did this happen?"

"About a month ago." Cheryl answered while twisting her hands.

"Has anything happened since then?"

"No."

Cheryl let the lie hang in the air and then decided to press on. "The only reason I came here is because now this is affecting my kids."

"Correction, it has always affected your kids, it's only now that you realize how much it has affected you kids."

"What is that supposed to mean? I am a damn good mother and I never let him touch them."

"I didn't say that you were a bad mother. Funny you say you never let him touch them. Well what about the mental abuse?"

"Maybe this wasn't the best idea for me to come here. I think I should be going." Cheryl grabbed her purse from the floor and stood up quickly.

"Ms. Bookman, please take a seat. I didn't mean to upset you. Let's start again." She said while rising and stepping in front of the door.

"I need to go. It's getting late and I need to get home to Kayla."

"Ok, I will let you go under one condition. That you return next week and we can talk a little more." She said as she moved back behind her desk, picked up a pen and a notepad.

"Maybe." Cheryl said.

"Ms. Bookman, please. I want your promise that you will come back to see me within the next couple of weeks."

"Ok." Cheryl said, taking the note from Linda's hand and stuffing it in her pocket.

Matthew arrived at his ex-wife's house and used the key to enter through the kitchen. She called and wanted to talk to him, yet she had the nerve not to answer the door. He knew she should be here since her car was in the driveway.

He walked in and smelled cigarette smoke.

"Sherrie, are you awake yet?" He yelled while staring into the almost empty refrigerator.

"Damn, what time is it?" She said while walking into the kitchen while pulling her robe on.

"You told me to come over around eight." He said as he pulled the bottle of orange juice from the door.

"I know what time I told you to come over, I didn't ask you that." She said as she rubbed the crust from the corner of her eye.

"I guess you haven't had your coffee yet." He said while filling the carafe with water and putting four heaping scoops of Maxwell House in the filter. He took the creamer from the refrigerator and sat it on the counter. "Let me ask you something, what the hell happened to your mouth."

"Nothing." She said while turning away from him and putting her hand to her face.

"Really?" he said while walking towards her and pulling her hand away. Her lip was swollen and bruised. "Well it wasn't like that last night when I was here, so either you hit your own self in the mouth or you got into a fight with someone, either way don't lie to me and tell me that you did this to yourself. Who hit you Sherrie?"

"Look, that's not why you are here...move so I can get some water." She said while pushing against him and pulled a glass from the overhead cabinet.

"Look, did something happen last night when I left."

She pushed her hands into her hair and pulled a rubber band from her robe pocket and put it around her shoulder length hair. She sat down and suddenly she was in tears. She wiped her face hard and stood.

"He hit me."

"Who?"

"Malcolm."

"Who the fuck is Malcolm?" He said while beginning to pace back and forth.

She stood and made her way to the sink and started rinsing out her cup.

"You don't need to raise your voice." She said.

"Like hell I don't! Who in the fuck you got coming up in here and letting them put their fucking hands on you!"

"Look if you gonna keep yelling, get the hell out! I am not in the mood for this shit this morning!"

She walked past Matthew and took out another cup. He grabbed the cup from her hand and slammed it on the counter, causing it to break into small pieces all over the floor. She got the broom from the pantry and starting sweeping.

"Look, stop cleaning and tell me what happened. Who is Malcolm and why would he hit you?"

"I don't think he meant..."

"Wait, don't start that bullshit with me. I deal with it from Cheryl, please don't start defending a nigga putting his hands on you."

"I wasn't. I was going to say he made a comment that I felt was inappropriate and I hit him and he swung back."

"What comment?"

"That doesn't matter. All that matters is, I won't be seeing him again *and* he will most likely be sitting in jail later."

"Good. That's all I want to hear."

"What do you think about Tamia coming to stay with me?"

"Are you crazy! She ain't going nowhere near that crazy ass bitch you are seeing."

"You need to slow your roll."

"You're the one needing to slow your roll. You come up in

here and tell me that you are taking Tamia. You are fucking crazy!"

"I didn't say anything about taking her from you. I am only suggesting that you let me take Tamia for a while. She says that…"

"What! What does she say?"

"Well, you got some nigga running up in here and putting their hands on you and then she isn't that crazy about whatever your new man's name is."

"Look nigga, you don't run shit up in here and neither does she. So you can get that out of head."

"I'm just saying…"

She got up from the table and slammed the cup on the counter, "You sure know how to spoil a nice visit with bullshit. Get the hell out!"

"Wait. Why don't we ask Tamia what she would like?"

"Are you fucking kidding me? That bitch doesn't make any fucking decisions in my house."

"Well, will you bring her over later and we can talk more about this."

"Aint shit to talk about. She aint coming to stay with you and that is final. Now, if you want her for the weekend, I'll send her over, but don't try anything, because I will have your ass back in court before you can blink."

"Well, are you going to bring her over, or should I send a car?"

"I'll bring her over when she gets back *and* I get a little more rest. Let yourself out." She said as she walked back towards her room.

"Good morning beautiful." Matthew said as Cheryl sat on the edge of her bed.

"Morning." She muttered as she rose from the bed and

154

walked to the bathroom. He heard the shower come on and after almost thirty minutes, she emerged with her hair pinned and water dripping down her legs. She pulled the towel around her tighter and sat on the bed while she poured oil in her hands and smoothed it over her caramel skin.

"I talked to Sherrie."

"How did that go?"

"Like I figured it would. She doesn't want Tamia coming to stay with me."

"Why?"

"Probably because she thinks she will lose the money I shell out in child support every month."

"How much do you pay?"

"The court order says twelve hundred, but I give her an extra two hundred just in case Tamia needs things for school."

"Damn, well she has a money tree in Tamia."

"Yeah, well, if she doesn't start taking better care of her then I will take her totally and not give a damn about her."

"Well, what is stopping you?"

"I am trying to give Sherrie the benefit of the doubt. She keeps on pushing me though. Do you know she let some nigga beat the shit out of her last night?"

"How do you know?"

"Her mouth is jacked up. She said that they had some kind of argument and he hit her after she hit him. I'll tell you what though, if I find out who did that to her, I'll teach him a lesson."

"Well, she is a grown woman..."

"What the hell does that mean?"

Cheryl held her hands up, "Well, wait a minute. I was just saying that you can't fight everyone's battle for them."

"I'm not trying to fight everyone's battle for them. I'm just sick of you women letting nigga's beat up on you."

"What in the hell does that mean, you women?"

155

"Nothing, damn, I didn't come over here to argue with you too."

"Look, you are the one that got all indignant when I asked you a simple question."

"Why don't we just end this conversation?"

"You know, you're right. Let's end this before someone gets their feelings hurt." Cheryl said as she folded her arms.

"Yeah, because I don't want to hurt yours." he mumbled under his breath.

"What the hell did you just say?"

"Calm the hell down. I didn't say anything." He opened her balcony door and stepped outside the warm room.

"No...you explain to me what the hell you meant, you don't want to hurt *my* feelings. Oh, so when you say some fucked up shit, you get to walk away. If I was to do the same thing, you would be all up in my damn face."

"Ok, you want to hear it!" He said while whirling around to face her. "You are the one with the ex-husband still beating the shit out of you whenever he feels like it. You are the one with the fucking daughter who is so fucking disrespectful, she should have a full set of false teeth in her mouth, because she sure as hell wouldn't be talking to me any kind of way. You are the one with the son who is as gay as all outdoors, and screwing some damn transvestite and you are the one with your head in the clouds like everything is ok. I try and help you and all I get is slapped in the fucking face for it. I try..."

"No! What you're trying to do is re-live your life through me by "saving" me from myself. I guess I should be grateful that you took time from your boring ass life to come and help little ole me! You know what, you're right, maybe you need to roll on, because you definitely have started my day off wrong!" she started to walk away but came back, "and no, my head is not in the clouds! I know my son is gay, but that is my business. I don't need to announce that to everyone, and how I take care of my daughter is my business, not yours. So if my children are a problem for you, then you should have said so, way before now. Not everyone can have a child that is stuck up and snobbish like you!" She quickly walked away and he was right behind her.

He followed her to the kitchen as she poured herself more coffee. She sat the carafe back into the coffeemaker and turned around. He stood so close to her that she bumped into him.

"If you don't mind, I need to get ready. I have a busy day. You can let yourself out." she walked upstairs and slammed her bedroom door shut.

Just then the phone rang and she let out a stream of curse words that would have made her mother blush.

Chapter 31

She got to Red Feather Charter School in about thirty minutes and saw the familiar grey Mercedes SUV with the vanity plates BLKSXS. Cheryl walked down to the hall to the main office and signed in on the computer and showed her id to Mrs. Briscoe.

"Good morning honey. How are things going?" said the chirpy young woman watering the plants behind the counter.

"Things would be better if I didn't have a little delinquent." She said with a sad smile and quick laugh. "How long has her dad been here?"

"You just missed him. He just walked around the corner to Ms. Christie's office."

As Cheryl rounded the corner, she heard him before she saw him.

"Look, I am about sick of being called because you can't seem to find your way to school. Where do you think you were going?"

Cheryl opened the door and all eyes were on her. "Yes I would like to know the answer to that question also."

Kayla didn't speak to either of them, instead directing her question to the principal, "Am I going to be suspended? It's not like I am the only one leaving school."

Cheryl yanked her daughter from the chair.

"You look here young lady, we are not talking about your little friends, we are talking about you and right now, you need to worry about whether *you* will be here next year, or in public school, since you don't seem to appreciate that your dad is paying for you to get the best education you can."

Kayla snatched her arm from her mother and backed up against the file cabinet in the corner. Kevin took a step and Ms. Christie came from behind her desk.

"Why don't we all just have a seat and let's talk about this calmly." She led Kayla to the chair on the left side of her desk, Cheryl took the seat in front of the desk and Kevin stood in the spot Kayla vacated.

"Although she is frequently late, this is the first time that we have caught Kayla trying to leave school grounds, so this would only be a half day suspension, however, I also wanted to talk to you about her grades."

Kayla rolled her eyes to the top of her head.

Ms. Christie continued, "She never turned in her signed report card."

"What report card?" Cheryl asked, "I remember signing the last one."

She started flipping through the files on her desk and pulled out the paper.

"This is her home room folder. In here are the copies and the day they were signed. I do not see one for her."

"What did you do with it?" Cheryl asked her daughter.

Kayla shrugged her shoulders.

"Can I see the copy?" Her father asked.

She put the copy on the desk in front of them.

"There has to be a mistake. Did they just get this?"

"As you can see by the date, they were issued last Monday, but she hasn't brought back the copy, and I can guess why."

"What in the hell is this?" Kevin shouted.

"My report card." Kayla whispered.

"I can't hear you."

"My report card." Kayla said a little louder.

"Why in the hell do you have three F's and a D young lady?"

"I don't know." Kayla said with attitude.

"Don't you dare..." Kevin was pulling her up out of the chair.

"Uh, Mr. Goldman, please, let's talk about this." Ms. Christie said while jumping up from her seat.

"Oh, we will be talking about this, at home!" Kevin pulled her from the office and pushed her in the hallway.

Cheryl grabbed the report card and tried not looking at Ms. Christie.

Ms. Christie spoke softly, "Is everything going to be ok when you get home? I mean, are you and Kayla going to be safe?"

Their eyes met and Cheryl tried to break the gaze, but Ms. Christie held her eyes hostage.

She spoke a little louder this time, "Cheryl, are you and Kayla going to be safe?"

"We don't live with him anymore."

"I didn't ask you that."

"Don't worry. We will be ok." She said and patted the woman's arm.

"Wait." She said and walked back to her desk. "Take this, it's my cell phone number, if you need it." She pressed her card into her hand and squeezed.

Cheryl assured the woman that they would be fine, but if she needed it, she would call. As Cheryl walked into the hallway, she saw her daughter flinch and quickened her pace towards them.

"You ungrateful little bitch, you have the fucking nerve to have an attitude and you are standing here with F's on your report card. You just wait until you get home, if your mother wasn't out here tramping around, she would have known what in the hell you were doing. That's ok though, because after today, you will think twice about coming to school late, leaving early or getting bad grades." Kevin said while grabbing her by the upper arm.

"Keep your damn hands off of her." Cheryl said, trying to keep her voice low. "I will deal with her myself and call you later."

She pulled Kayla through the front doors of the school and towards her vehicle. They climbed in, in silence and drove home. They walked into the house and Kayla started for the steps

"You have a lot of explaining to do!"

"Whatever." Kayla said and starting walking up the stairs.

"What did you just say to me?"

"You heard me!" Kayla said while turning around on the third step.

"You better watch your tone young lady. I am about sick of your mess! You are getting disrespectful."

Kayla turned and continued walking up the stairs.

"I didn't tell you to go anywhere." Cheryl said as she started up the steps behind her daughter and grabbed her shirt.

"Get your hands off of me!" Kayla said as she turned around.

Chapter 32

Monday came and the office was busier than ever. Alpine Spa and M & T Limo Service had been on board for about two months now and they had steered more business their way than the commercials they shelled twelve hundred dollars a month out for.

Rebecca was on the phone all morning talking to the people in Atlanta. She got off of the phone and he overheard her telling Ashley to have her itinerary ready in the next few minutes.

"I'll be taking Toni with me when I go to Atlanta." She said as she walked into his office, unannounced.

"Good morning to you too." he said while turning his chair away from the window.

"Did you hear what I said?"

"I did, and who said that Toni would be going to Atlanta? I didn't approve her travel."

"Oh, so now travel has to be approved? Since when did this *little* arrangement start?"

"I think you came in here with the wrong attitude. What is your problem?" he said while rising from his chair and walking towards his door.

Rebecca rolled her eyes and blew out a hard breath, "I guess you change the rules whenever you feel like it, huh? This is my office and I don't need to check with you for anything."

At the reference of 'her' office, he corrected her, "you mean my office."

"Oh, it's like that?" she said while shifting her weight from one foot to the other.

"It's always been like that, and I think we had this discussion before." he said while picking up his glass and sitting down on the caramel colored chair.

"No, we didn't discuss anything. As far as I knew, that office was mine. You said it before it was open, you said it at the grand opening and you said it when I managed to sign that artist from DC. Do you think I would have spent all of that time in Atlanta, doing all that work, if I didn't think that office was mine?"

"Yes, because you *work* for *me*. Just like Corey is in New York *running* that office, you are *running* the office in Atlanta, and I am running the office here in DC. You never hear Corey say that the New York office is his, do you?"

"Did you tell him the office wasn't his?"

"This is my company and I don't have to answer to you, nor him."

"I thought you and Corey owned it fifty, fifty?"

"We do, and Corey knows his place in this company. When *we* started this company, twenty years ago we knew we would eventually expand."

"So does Corey know that he doesn't own any stock in the other two offices?"

"Ok, and again, let me say this, that is none of your business. You are running the Atlanta office and since you don't like doing that, then maybe I need to look at making a change."

"What the hell does that mean?"

"You might want to back up and slow your roll or you might need to find yourself…"

"Let me tell you one fucking thing, *Mr*. Goldman. Don't you ever fucking threaten me. I won't need to *find* shit because this is where I plan on staying. Now you might want to rethink your position, because that little *incident* we had a few weeks ago, has not been forgotten. Remember I told you that I had spoken with someone about it, well what I didn't tell you, I also have documented the injuries that *you* caused. Now don't for one fucking minute believe that what you did to that bitch ex-wife of yours will be happening with me. My name isn't Cheryl and I don't play that shit! Now like I said earlier, *Toni* and I will be going to Atlanta on Wednesday. I'll have Ashley give you the itinerary as soon as I have it finalized." She said as she turned on her red bottom shoes and marched out of his office. Kevin was left sitting in his office with his jaws tight and a major headache moving in.

Chapter 33

Cheryl adjusted her sunglasses and walked in. Matthew was hovering over the realtor's shoulder. She didn't know that she could be jealous but in that instance she was.

She cleared her throat as she stood in the doorway, "Hello, I'm so sorry I'm late."

"Hello beautiful." He said as he walked over to her.

She sidestepped him, "What have I missed?"

The realtor didn't look up when she spoke, "Nothing, I was just showing Matthew the new property that you wanted the specs on. It is still available, but not for long. Another agent called me this morning and said that she was taking a client to see it.

"Well can we still see it?" Cheryl asked.

"Sure. Can you go now?"

"Uh, yes, just let me make a phone call and I'll be right with you." Cheryl said as she turned and headed back to the door.

"Great. Do you want to drive or shall we car pool." Sharon said as she printed out the address and stood.

"We'll drive." Matthew spoke up.

"Sharon, can you point me to your bathroom. I need to freshen up." Cheryl said as she walked past Matthew.

"First door on the left."

"Thanks, I'll be right out." she said and quickly pulled out her cell phone. Cheryl quickly went into why she couldn't come for her counseling session but promised that she would call and make another appointment soon.

"Everything ok in there?" Matthew asked from behind the closed door.

She flushed the unused toilet and washed her hands.

"What happened?" Matthew asked.

"Do you really want to know all of the details?" she said with a weak smile.

"You know what I am talking about." Matthew said.

"Are you two ready?" Sharon asked.

"Yep." Cheryl answered, walking around the corner of the office.

They walked out and Matthew guided her to his truck.

"It is going to be about a twenty minute ride." Sharon said as she pulled up beside them.

"No problem." he said "that gives you twenty minutes to explain what in the hell happened."

"Look, I don't have to explain anything to you."

"Like hell you don't. You are the one who set up this meeting, and then you waltz up in here almost a half hour late and you don't say what the hell is going on. Then you have on glasses and haven't taken them off since you got here. Now, if there isn't a good excuse to have them on, then take them off."

"Look, I had an eye appointment today and they dilated my eyes, so my eyes are a little sensitive, ok. Damn, I didn't think I had to tell you everything."

"Ok, sorry." he said and tried to hold her hand, but Cheryl pulled it away.

Her phone rang and she spoke to Donnell, asking him to stay with Kayla until she arrived home.

"Problem with Kayla?"

"Not that you need to be concerned about." she said with a wave of her hand.

"What does that mean?"

Cheryl rolled her eyes to the top of her head, "Nothing. Can you stop talking, I have a headache."

Matthew started to say something but instead he turned the radio to the jazz station and kept his mouth shut.

He walked into the outer office and heard Ashley finishing up the travel plans for Rebecca and Toni. Then he asked her what time they were leaving.

Kevin turned and headed towards Rebecca's office where he overheard them talking about the trip.

This time it was he, who walked in, unannounced. "Do you have everything that I asked you to have ready?" he said to Toni.

"Almost"

"Almost?" he said with an attitude. As she started to explain, he interrupted her and told her he needed to talk to Rebecca.

"I'm busy." Rebecca said as he dismissed Toni.

"Who in the hell do you think you are?" Kevin said as he walked over to her desk. "I think you better remember who you are dealing with."

"I already know who I am dealing with. You are the nigga that thinks you are going to go back on your word about the Atlanta office."

"I'm also the nigga that signs your fucking paychecks." he said while walking behind her desk and standing in front of her.

She stood up, "Let me tell you one…"

He grabbed her upper arm, "No let me tell you something. You don't ever threaten me. Do you understand me? I don't want to have to hurt you, so you better remember who the fuck you are dealing with."

"Get your hands…"

"No, see I think you are still forgetting." he said while tightening his grip. "I would hate to show you how I handle bitches like you."

"Oh, is that how you kept Cheryl under your thumb?"

"That is none of your business."

"Really, why don't I refresh *your* memory? Remember when you raped your wife and I came and helped you clean up your shit? Let's see if I can help you remember something else. How about when you went to see her in the hospital and you went into her room and she told you that she lost the baby because of what you had done to her? You didn't think I heard that did you? Well, I'll tell you what, it's not a fucking threat, it's a promise. You will *give* me the Atlanta office, or you will be the one sorry my friend. Now take your fucking hands off of me." She said as she snatched her arm free.

"Yes, I think I would be able to pull off the asking price, but I don't want to offer it right off. See if they will take twenty percent less and then give me a call later." Cheryl told Sharon as they walked back towards their parked vehicles.

Once in the car, Matthew turned to Cheryl.

"Ok, so can I ask you a question without you biting my head off?"

"Sure."

"Why do you still have on those glasses when the sun went down almost an hour ago? The dilation should have worn off by now?"

"Are you serious?"

"Deadly, and I am not moving this truck until you tell me or you remove the glasses."

His phone rang, saving her from telling him another lie. He told her that his daughter would be staying at his house and she steered the conversation in that direction.

"We should get going. Do you need to stop and get anything? I really need to get home to Kayla. I have left her to her own devices long enough today."

As they pulled up in front of the realtor's office, Cheryl quickly unbuckled and got out of the truck and made her way over to Sharon.

"Please make sure you call me whenever you hear anything."

"I sure will. You have a great evening." Sharon said.

"Thank you, I will." Cheryl walked to her car and got in. As she was about to shut the door, Matthew held it open.

"Do you honestly think you are going to go anywhere without answering my question?"

"Matthew, come on. Now what does it matter? I told you earlier, I had an eye appointment, no big deal."

He reached for her glasses.

She put her hands on her glasses, "Matthew, will you please. I really need to get going."

"Ok, but trust and believe I am not letting this go. I expect an explanation."

"And I expect my offer to be accepted, but we don't always get what we expect." she said while closing her door, putting the car in drive and leaving him there.

Matthew picked up his daughter and was enjoying spending time with her. His job was so busy that he didn't like that she was growing up so fast. He walked into her room and saw her on the computer.

"Hey baby girl. What 'cha doing?"

"Nothing, just on my *Facebook* page."

"Yeah, let me see who you have as friends."

She sucked her teeth which caused an instant reaction from him.

"Ah, I know I didn't just hear you suck your teeth young lady. Now, either you let me see, or I will make sure that you don't have access to the internet again. Do I make myself clear?"

"Yes sir."

He turned her computer around and started scrolling through the pictures.

"Who is this?" he said as he pointed to the young woman on the screen.

"Dad, are you serious?"

"Yeah, why?"

"You don't know who that is?" she said with a look of disbelief on her face.

"Tamia, no I don't, now just tell me who it is, you know I hate guessing games."

"That's Kayla."

The young girl had on a bikini, on her hands and knees with her tongue licking her lips. The makeup tried to hide the young features but you knew if you stared at the picture long enough that girl was way too young for the men that she probably fooled with those pictures.

Matthew did a double take on the next picture.

"Who the hell is this?" he said pointing at the screen.

"That's Mr. Malcolm."

"No baby girl, I'm talking about this guy." he said while pointing to the picture. "Yeah, that's Mr. Malcolm, mom's friend."

"What the hell!" he raced back into his bedroom and grabbed the cell phone off of the nightstand and called Sherrie. After ringing four times, it went to voice mail.

Chapter 34

Kevin turned his computer on and sat back in his chair with his drink in his hand and the computer glowing back at him.

Kissmehard: hey sexy.

Suxcesblkman: hey yourself.

Kissmehard: what r u up 2

Suxcesblkman: nuttin

Kissmehard: r u up 4 sum fun

Suxcesblkman: not 2nite

Kissmehard: WTF!!! clutch the pearls lol

Suxcesblkman: I am not n the mood

Kissmehard: well I am

Suxcesblkman: I'm sure u can find sum1 2 play wit

Kissmehard: I want u

Suxcesblkman: well I want 2 talk

Kissmehard: whazzup

Suxcesblkman: I think I made a mistake dat bitch tryn 2 take my company

Kissmehard: ? Cheryl?

Suxcesblkman: no, RH

Kissmehard: didn't I tell u to watch that trick?

Suxcesblkman: yea, but u know…lol

Kissmehard: yea…she probly sucked ur dick or sum shit and had u sprung

Suxcesblkman: sumthan like dat

Kissmehard: LMAO I took n tole u

Suxcesblkman: not took n tole….lmao

Kissmehard: dat's more like it

Suxcesblkman: yeah, I knew I could count on u

Kissmehard: yep, c I know what my boo likes

Suxcesblkman: yes u do. Now come give me what I like

Kissmehard: oooo..u so nassy.

Suxcesblkman: & u like it, don't u. now open up, let daddy give u sumthan

Kissmehard: oooo its so big…mmmm..Mmmm

Suxcesblkman: Ssssss…yea…suc it baby

Kissmehard: mmmm….I can taste ur cum on da tip

Suxcesblkman: mmmm deep throat me baby

Kissmehard: mmmm..

Suxcesblkman: turn a round

Kissmehard: oooo daddy…I'm on my nees

Suxcesblkman: …ummmm mmmm mmmm mmmm….shit..my dick is so hard

Kissmehard: give it 2 me daddy…yes….yes….grab my ass….yes…yesss

Suxcesblkman: shit….u want me 2 cum baby

Kissmehard: yes..Oh yes….I want 2 cum 2 baby..yes..

Suxcesblkman: yea…yea…. …yea mmmm

Kissmehard: oh yea….

Suxcesblkman: shit…

Kissmehard: yeah daddy…Ahhh ooooo…yessssss…..

Suxcesblkman: shit….I needed that…I gotta run clean up…brb

Kissmehard: take ur time. I need a cig…

Kevin logged off and headed into the shower in his office. As the hot water rinsed away the last few minutes, his mind turned to his childhood.

Kevin had walked to his friend's house after another episode with Henry. He heard them from the backroom telling Mike's mother what was going on. Well their version of it anyway.

"Look, he got out of line so I beat his ass. That is how you have to bring these kids back in check. If not, they will try and run all over you."

"Henry!" he heard his mother call, but he wasn't moving from his spot in the closet.

"I'm sorry if he caused you any problems. Kevin! Kevin! Get out here." Kevin's mother said.

After a few minutes of debating with himself, Kevin came out and walked over to his mom and wrapped his small arms around her waist.

"Mom, I'm sorry."

"Oh sweetie, it's ok. Let's go home and I will make your favorite dinner, ok."

He took his mother's hand but noticed the hate dripping from Henry's face like sweat.

They walked in and immediately Henry slapped his mother across the face and accused her of embarrassing him in front of Mike's mom. His mom didn't say anything, she just held her face and then Henry started punching her like she was a rag doll. Kevin's mom fell into a heap on the floor and then it was his turn. He dragged Kevin into his room and threw him across the bed. Kevin finally got free and was able to flip over and Henry's face was contorted like he was in pain and his penis was spewing liquid all over him. He was in a different world. He was mumbling something about bringing them back in line and teaching them a lesson, when suddenly he started turning blue and he fell over. Kevin scrambled to the door and let his mom in and she went over to him and then she came back to Kevin and led him out of the bedroom. Thirty minutes later the paramedics came and said that Henry had died. They said something about a massive coronary and that he didn't suffer.

Kevin and his mom moved from that apartment a month later

and soon his mom said she was *seeing* Henry. She couldn't go to work anymore, because she thought some of the customers were Henry. One day while leaving work, she ran back into the restaurant and locked herself in the deep freezer because she said Henry was outside waiting for her.

The day that Henry died, mom could have helped him, but she told her son not to call 911 until she told him to, which was after she went in the room, put his clothes back on him, gave Kevin a shower and then washed her face. She told him not to ever say anything to anyone about what happened that day. One day Kevin came home from school and she was hanging from the banister.

Chapter 35

"Cheryl I'm so glad you called. I was worried when you missed our appointment today. Is everything ok?"

"No it isn't. Today my daughter hit me."

"Are you ok?"

"Yes, just a sore face and headache, but she actually told my son that she would do it again, if I get in her face. I was trying to discipline…"

"Why are you explaining it to me?"

"I wasn't, I was just…"

"You were just trying to defend your actions. I am sure you did that with Kevin also."

"But…"

"I'm not Kevin, and everything doesn't have to be explained. What needs to be explained is why your daughter felt it is ok to hit you. You remember when you told me that your kids weren't affected by the violence in your marriage? I guess you can see that you were wrong, they have been. Kayla felt it was ok to hit you, just like Kevin did while you were married. First, you need to address your daughter and let her know that hitting you is not acceptable. Have you thought of family counseling?"

"No, Kevin…"

"What does Kevin have to do with this?"

"He doesn't want Kayla talking to anyone."

"Does Kayla live with you or him?"

"Me."

"So, you are telling me that you are going to let him run your household also."

"No."

"Ok, well I know of a nice family counselor here at the center and I will pass on your information. Now, what time is good for you tomorrow?"

"I can't…"

"Cheryl, you have to meet this head on. Now tomorrow I have an opening at eleven and one, which one would you like?"

"Eleven." She said reluctantly.

"Great, see you then. Have a good evening, ok. Tomorrow is a new day."

Cheryl hung up and called her friend Dee. After some small talk she told Dee about her Kayla hitting her.

"I hope you beat that ass!" Dee screamed into the phone.

"I…"

"Cheryl, I know you are not about to tell me that you didn't handle that."

Dee announced that she was on her way to Cheryl's house before Cheryl could protest.

Chapter 36

Dee raced down the stairs behind Cheryl. She found her standing in the kitchen with pools of water forming in her eyes.

"What the hell was that?" She asked.

"That is what I deal with on a daily basis."

Dee sucked her teeth and pulled the chair out from the table, "Why? That little girl upstairs should be picking her damn teeth up off of the floor."

"Everything can't be solved by hitting." Cheryl said as she joined her friend at the table.

"Like hell it can't. It might not be solved, the answer would be crystal clear." She said as she folded her arms across her large breasts.

"Are you clueless that your daughter is crying out for help, or at the very least, a good ass whopping?"

"Look, I might not be the best parent in the world, but I am not going to hit her every time she speaks her mind."

"Are you fucking serious? Maybe you haven't looked in the mirror at your black eye. Why in the hell would you let a 15 year old do that? You let that jackass do it for years, and now you are handing over the gloves to Kayla. That ass would be beat down if my child…"

"That's just it Dee, she isn't your child." Cheryl said as she rose from the table.

"But she is my god-daughter, and that counts as my child."

"Dee, I have already called the counselor."

"Was this before or after you tore her a brand new one."

"No, Donnell came over and talked to her."

"Why in the hell is Donnell talking to her, instead of you? You are her damn mother. Cheryl, please don't let her do this. Don't let your child pick up where Kevin left off."

"I won't."

"But you already have, the minute she raised her hand to you, you should have handled it, but instead, you let Donnell handle it. What does that show Kayla?"

Dee rose from the table and blew out a breath, "That girl has everything that she could ever want, and you are kissing her ass."

Cheryl turned quickly "OK, now wait a minute. I am not kissing anything, I'm just trying to make sure that she knows that I am always..."

"You might not be kissing it, but you sure as hell are licking all around it. You are sending her the message that you don't care if she treats you like Kevin did, and nothing will happen to her, again, just like Kevin. I thought you were in counseling?"

"I am."

"What does your counselor say about this?" Dee took another breath, "you didn't tell her, did you? Jesus Christ...look, you better not let this girl get away with that...do you hear me? I love you and I don't want you to think you are in this alone. I am here, no matter what. Ok?" she said as she gave her friend a hug.

Matthew was handcuffed and placed in the back of the police cruiser. Sherrie was left standing in front of the restaurant and Malcolm was being put on a stretcher.

He arrived at the detention center and went through the process he had just endured less than two weeks before.

"Back again." Said the female officer with too much makeup on.

He was led to a holding cell, was told that he would see the magistrate in about an hour.

After looking at his papers a few more times, the magistrate decided he would let Matthew go on a fifteen thousand dollar cash bond.

Matthew was able to call his lawyer and have the money in less than an hour but it still took three hours to get him released.

He was released and went to Cheryl's house. Just as he was about to knock on the door, it came flying open and Kayla was in full trot.

"I told you that you could not go!" Cheryl called out behind her daughter.

"And I said that I had already planned on going over there to finish my project. Dang, I'm only going to be gone for a couple of hours".

"Kayla, I'm serious…" she said as her daughter continued walking down the street.

Matthew walked up, gave a look and a quick kiss.

"What in the hell? Why is Kayla running out of here like the house is on fire?"

Cheryl collapsed into his arms in tears.

Her words came rushing out as if a faucet had been turned on and she couldn't hold them back.

Matthew led her into the house, kicking the door shut and guiding her to the sofa, "Slow down and calm yourself down before your asthma kicks in."

"She is getting out of control." She was gulping in air as if she had just surfaced from underwater. "I try and give her everything…"

"Maybe that's the problem. I am not the expert on parenting by any means, but I do know that Tamia will never, ever talk to me the way that Kayla talks to you."

She jumped from sofa, "Well, I am not going to spank her like she is a baby."

"I'm not telling you to do that, I'm suggesting that you give her consequences. There is no way in hell she would have been leaving this house after what she did. Do you know where she went?"

"No, she didn't say." Cheryl said as she held her head down.

"That's another thing, she is not twenty five, she is fifteen, and she needs to tell you where she goes when she leaves this house. Cheryl, let's try and think where she would go and then you need to go and get your daughter."

Kayla called her dad.

"Dad can you come and get me?"

"For what?" he asked very annoyed that his nap was interrupted.

"Mom is tripping."

"Talk English."

"Mom hit me." She said with as much emotion as she could muster.

"What? I'm on my way." He said as the torrent of curse words flooded the air.

He barely allowed Cheryl to open the door before he began speaking.

"I came to get my daughter."

Cheryl walked behind him.

"Oh, so now she is your daughter. Well, I think you were the one who said you didn't want to, and let me use your exact words, want that little bitch around you. I do believe that was less than a month ago. So she gets grounded and now she comes running to you."

Kevin took a step towards her, "Don't you fucking…"

"Slow your roll, "Matthew said as Kevin advanced around the coffee table towards Cheryl. "I would hate to have to deal with you again."

Cheryl stood and held her hand up, "I'll will handle this."

Matthew stopped short, turned and went to the front door. He spoke over his shoulder, "Call me when you need me." He said as he opened the front door and let it slam behind him.

Chapter 37

Sherrie looked at her phone.

"I have to take this call."

"Not while you are sitting here with me, you won't." Malcolm said.

"Look, it might be something wrong with Tamia." she said while picking it up and texting. She turned the phone off after sending the text and dropped it into her purse then ordered rum and coke. She thought this night was turning out to be more headache than it was worth.

She turned on her phone and it came alive with the texts from Matthew. She called him and he asked her where she was.

"None of your business." She practically yelled into the phone

"Look, I need you to tell me where you are. You might be in danger."

"Whatever. Look, do you want me to come and pick up Tamia?"

Matthew raised his voice "No. Look, I can't go into it over the phone, but you need to tell me where the hell you are."

She hung up, her mood was in the toilet because of her date and now her ex. She cursed out loud and as she exited the stall her phone rang again.

"Matthew, what do you want?"

"Tell me where you are. I think you are in danger."

"Whatever…"

"Sherrie. Listen to me. The man you are on a date with, I think I know him."

"Whatever." She said as she sucked her teeth.

Matthews's voice was so loud that the woman next to her raised her eyebrows. Her eyes got big and she gave him her location.

She walked back to the table and Malcolm was already gone. She felt someone grab her from behind.

"Ugh, you scared me." she said when she saw Malcolm.

"I thought you had fallen in since you took so long."

"Do you want to sit at the bar for a couple of drinks or something?" she said, trying to keep her voice from sounding shaky.

"No, I'm ready to get out of here, for dessert." he said while pulling her close to him.

"Well, let me grab something for dessert to take home for later." she said while moving away from him.

"Come on. I want to get out of here."

"Damn, can I at least get something for later? Don't worry, I have money for it."

He grabbed her quickly by the arm, "what the hell is that supposed to mean?"

"Nothing, and don't be causing no scene. I was just saying I wanted to take something home for Tamia because I told her I would. It won't take too long."

The commotion caught his attention immediately. He heard his ex-wife telling someone to take their hands off of her. He exited his truck and walked with a purpose towards the commotion. Matthew addressed Malcolm as he approached.

"Well, up to your old tricks I see." Matthew as the man held onto his ex-wife's arm.

183

Malcolm gave him a mischievous stare.

"Malcolm, so that's the name you are going by these days?" Matthew said as he walked closer.

Finally Malcolm spoke, "You are slipping my friend. I thought for sure you would have figured it out before now."

Matthew stepped closer to Malcolm and spoke just above a whisper, "Oh, how soon we forget. Tell you what, I'll give you a head start."

"As you can see I have a date." Malcolm said towards Sherrie.

"I'm surprised you see her, you know, with only *one* good eye."

"I seem to do ok, with this *one* eye. I snagged her didn't I?"

"They say that a dog is man's best friend."

The crowd grew bigger and bigger around them.

Malcolm was calm as he spoke "You can't seem to keep your women happy. If you weren't always working, you would have never left your momma alone and now, well you can see how much she is digging me."

Matthew pushed Malcolm away from Sherrie, "I'm not telling you again."

"Like I said, I'm on a date. Come on Sherrie." He said, grabbing her arm again.

Matthew dropped him with a blow to the side of the head. He walked away leaving the people gasping and yelling to call the police.

Dee had practically knocked the door down before Donnell came to the door.

"Where is your sister?" she said as she blew in like a hurricane.

"Upstairs." Donnell said stepping to the side.

She slammed open Kayla's door while yelling. "Who in the hell do you think you are?"

Hi Dee." She said as she got up from her bed.

"Have you lost your fucking mind?"

"What?"

"Don't give me that shit! You know exactly what I am talking about. Why in the hell are you hitting your mother?"

"She hit me."

She walked towards her dresser while Dee stood there with her hands on her hips.

Dee was shocked by the nonchalant attitude, "What did you just say?"

Dee's hard stare was met by Kayla's

"You better get it together missy, or unlike what your mother did, you will get your ass dealt with, now sit your ass down!"

Cheryl came into the room, "Dee, what are you doing?"

"Getting this Perra` straight."

"I didn't ask you to do that."

"No you didn't, but somebody has too. Obviously you all are walking around here letting this girl run wild. Where the hell have you been?" she said while pointing to Donnell.

"Look, you ain't got problems with me, it's Kayla in this mess. I'm out of it. See you later mom." he said while making a quick retreat from the room.

"Dee, this is not necessary, I have spoken…"

"Oh, you have spoken to her. Are you fucking serious? You need to handle this before she does it again."

"If she hits me again, I'm hitting her back." Kayla announced.

Dee snatched her up from her seat and slapped her upside her head.

"Don't you ever let me hear that shit come out of your mouth again…"

Kayla snatched away from her and yelled, "But...but she didn't have any right..."

"Young lady, she has every right, she is your mother."

"I wish she wasn't!"

Dee gasped and Cheryl turned and left the room. Kayla sat on the bed, inserted her ear plugs, and picked up her phone.

Chapter 38

"Why in the hell are you putting your hands on Kayla?" Kevin shouted before Cheryl had made her way back into the living room.

"Why are you yelling?" she said in almost a whisper.

"Because I can, answer the fucking question!" He shouted back at her.

"For the same reason you put your hands on me while we were married."

"Don't get cute with me!"

"This is my house and I will get cute when I want to!" Cheryl shouted to his back as he approached the steps leading to the bedrooms.

"You are such a piece of work! Kayla get down here!" Kevin said from the bottom of the steps.

"You just remember that she is still in my custody." Cheryl said standing behind him.

"Look, I am so sick of your smart ass!" he said as he spun around and grabbed her hair.

"Get your hands off of me, or I swear, I will call the police!"

The sting of his hand meeting her face was incredible. She pulled her cell from her pocket and hit the emergency key.

"Dad, come on." she heard Kayla say in a rushed voice as she bumped against her mother.

The doorbell rang and Cheryl rushed to open it. Two police

officers stood on her stoop.

"Is there a problem here ma'am?" the woman officer asked.

"Yes there is officer. My ex-husband came here to pick up my daughter…"

"Our daughter." he responded.

"And he assaulted me. I want him arrested." She continued.

The officer asked him to step outside.

"Not without my daughter." Kevin said.

"Sir, I am not going to ask you again." The female officer said.

Kevin immediately went into an explanation, "Look, I came over here, because she called me…"

"Who called you?" the second officer asked.

"My daughter."

"Why did she call you?"

"Her mother hit her and she has no right putting her hands on my daughter."

"So you came over here to do what?"

Kevin spoke quickly, "Not that it is any of your business, but I came over here to pick her up and take her to my house. My ex-wife was being difficult as I tried to take her, and I might add she has been drinking, and when we tried leaving she tried to prevent me from taking her."

"So what did you do?"

"Nothing, I told Kayla to come on and then you all showed up."

The female officer walked inside and motioned for Cheryl to follow her while Officer Colton waited with Kevin on the porch.

The officer looked at Cheryl and then turned her face to the side.

"Did he do that?"

Cheryl hesitated before answering yes and the officer walked away.

Matthew walked to the refrigerator and took out a PowerAde and headed to his bedroom to change into his workout clothes. As he headed downstairs his cell phone rang that familiar tone, which he ignored.

After twenty minutes of cardio and another hour weightlifting, he felt exhilarated. He walked into the shower, off of the workout room, and let the water slide down his body. He heard the doorbell, jumped from the shower and threw a towel around his waist to head upstairs.

"What in the hell is wrong? Is Tamia ok?" he said while ushering his ex-wife inside.

"Yes, it's just...."

"Look, calm down and let me get some clothes on, feel free to get yourself something to drink." he said as he stepped away from her. He ran up the stairs to his bedroom to put some clothes on. He came from his closet and saw Sherrie standing in his room

"Why are you in my room?" he asked her.

"I was..."

"Let's head back downstairs." he said while starting to walk by her.

"Matthew, can I have a hug?"

"Sure." he said as he pulled her close to him.

"I just want to say thank you for what you did for me today. I don't know what would have happened if you weren't so pushy."

"Who me, pushy, no way." he said into the top of her head.

"Uh, look. We shouldn't be doing this." he said while pushing her away.

"Don't you still want me?" she asked sadly.

"Look, let's sit..." before he could finish she had pressed her lips against his. As he pulled away, she gave him a pleading look and ran her hand under his t-shirt.

189

"Matthew, please. I just want you to hold me, is that too much to ask?"

"No, but I don't want you to get the wrong…"

"I know, I just needed to feel your touch. I'm sorry." she said as she moved towards the stairs and descended them.

Cheryl called one more person. When she didn't answer, she left a message and was led back to the cell.

Four hours went by and finally she was free to go. She walked out and Dee was there waiting for her.

Dee rushed up to Cheryl and wrapped her arms around her, "Please don't tell me you were in there crying like a damn baby."

"Well excuse me for being emotional. I'm not used to being locked up like a common criminal."

"Oh, like I am?" Dee said.

"I didn't say that."

"Look, now is not the time for us to be arguing. What in the hell are you in jail for?"

"Kevin had me arrested."

Dee stopped in her tracks and was rear-ended by a cute cop.

"Sorry miss." He said in his baritone voice.

"No apologies necessary." she said with a wink.

"Can you stop flirting long enough to hear my story?" Cheryl said with attitude.

"Well, little miss jail bird, don't get flip with me, you the one locked up." she said with her hand on her hips.

After hearing the story, Dee thought it was in injustice for them to arrest Cheryl for disciplining her child.

"They can if you leave marks on them. I didn't mean to. I guess my nails scratched her face and neck, so they arrested me on charges of child abuse. Then they said that social services would be contacting me and then they gave her to Kevin." The tears slid down faster.

"Cheryl, don't worry. It will be alright. You should have whooped that ass a long time ago, but don't beat yourself up about it. They will find out that you are a good mother and she will be home before you know it."

"You think so?"

"Sure, why not. You are not the one that has the anger issues. Why didn't you call Matthew?"

"I did, but he didn't answer. I guess he is mad with me too."

"What did you do now?"

"Why do you assume I did something to him?"

"He doesn't seem the type to walk out on you, especially after seeing you arrested."

They continued to Dee's car and got inside.

Cheryl continued talking after Dee got in.

"He didn't see me arrested. After Kevin got there and started acting all shitty towards me, Matthew got mad."

"Because you told him to mind his business?" she said to Cheryl while raising her eyebrow.

"I didn't tell him in those words, but he always wants to create a conflict when all I want is to let the situation die down."

"Did he hit Kevin?"

"No."

"So how do you know that it was going to be a conflict?"

"I don't. I'm just saying. Look I don't know what I am saying. Can you take me to Matthew's house?"

"If you want." Dee said and made a U-turn at the next corner and pointed her car in the direction of Matthew's house.

Chapter 39

Kayla walked in before her father did and threw her bag on the steps and went into the kitchen. Kevin asked her if she wanted to talk.

"Nope."

"Well, I think we should lay down some ground rules."

"Are you serious? I could have stayed at moms for all of this." she said while drinking her glass of grape juice.

"Now wait a minute. I think you remember what happened to you when you had a slick mouth before, I would hate to have to remind you."

"Tsk." She said

He stepped closer to her and she flinched.

"Now, I suggest we get some things clear. That little episode of skipping school will not be happening here, nor will you be coming and going as you please. Is that understood?"

She didn't answer.

"I'm sorry, I didn't hear you." he said and inched closer to her.

"Yes." She mumbled.

"Your curfew will be eleven o'clock on the weekdays and midnight on the weekends, understand?"

"Yes."

"Good and you will not be disrespectful when Rebecca comes over."

She rolled her eyes but answered yes anyway. "Can I go now?"

"Yes. There is some Neosporin in the bathroom cabinet, go put some on your face." he said as she walked away from him.

Kevin made a drink and called Rebecca.

"Hey baby."

"Hey yourself." She answered back.

"Look, I'm sorry for this afternoon."

"Ok."

"Well, you up for some company?"

"Nope." Rebecca answered dryly.

"I said I was sorry."

"I heard you."

"So you are still going to stay mad."

"I ain't mad."

"Then I'll see you in about an hour." Kevin hung up and went to grab a shower.

He told Kayla he would be back, but if all worked out, he didn't plan on coming back until after work tomorrow. He felt he was overdue for some alone time with Rebecca.

Kevin pulled into Rebecca's garage and touched the hood of her car. The car was cool signaling to him that hadn't gone anywhere lately. He walked in, nodded to her doorman and headed to the fifth floor.

"Hey sexy." he say to her while pulling her close and pushing his tongue inside her mouth before she could speak.

She broke the kiss, "Look Kevin. I think we need to clear the air about some things that were said."

"Come on baby. Let's talk later. As you can tell, I'm in the mood, and talking isn't what I had in mind."

"I'm serious, we need to get some things straight."

"What things?"

193

"The Atlanta…"

"I'm not discussing that tonight."

"I think we need to."

"Look, we already discussed it. You know my position on it and I am not changing my mind." he said, while sitting on her couch.

"I think…"

"I said we are not discussing it. I didn't come over here to hear this bullshit tonight."

"Well, I didn't tell you to bring your ass over here. I told you I wasn't in the mood."

"Look, let's just chill and have a nice time.".

"Kevin, look I'm serious. You said some things in the office that I can't let go, namely that you were looking for someone to run the Atlanta office."

He jumped from the sofa and started pacing back and forth. "And again, let me say this to you, you took the time to do what was necessary for us to open another office, you didn't complain when I was writing you those expense checks."

"You wrote those checks because I had *expenses.*"

"Seriously, you're going to tell me that you spent eight thousand dollars on work expenses?"

"I spent eight thousand dollars to make sure that I had a damn place to stay while I was there and let's not even talk about I had to eat while I was there."

"Oh right, and you spent six thousand dollars to *eat*? Tell me something else."

"This is not even about that, this is about me taking over the Atlanta office, like you promised me."

"I didn't promise you anything, and for you to say that I did, would be a flat out lie."

"Are you calling me a liar?"

"Look you need to back down. I didn't call you anything, all I said was…"

"All you said was that I was lying about the expenses. I don't appreciate that shit! You are the one who is a liar!" she said while pointing her finger in his face.

"What the fuck did you just say to me?" he said as he slapped it away.

"You heard what the hell I said, you are a liar! I guess that's why your dumb ass ex-wife kept staying with your trifling ass!"

He grabbed her arms and pulled her towards him. As she struggled against him, he raised his fist and slammed it into her face.

He was sweating and he had a few scratches but he left her where she lay.

Chapter 40

Dee pulled her car up behind the car already parked in Matthew's driveway and commented about him having company.

"Just the ex-wife." Cheryl answered.

"Well I suggest you go in there and let her know that he is *your* man."

"Be serious Dee, I am not worried about her."

Dee put her car in park and turned in her seat, "Let me tell you something, I don't care who the woman is, you never say you aren't worried about another woman with your man, especially if that woman used to be his wife. Hell, she knows his weaknesses and his strengths."

"Whatever." Cheryl opened the door, only half listening to Dee.

She rang the doorbell and Sherrie opened it.

Cheryl spoke but got no reply. Dee came walking up behind her and heard Sherrie comment about them coming to see 'her' man.

Dee saw Matthew first.

"What's up Matthew? Guess what, your girl went and got herself locked up today." she said with a laugh.

"Dee, damn, I was going to tell him once we were in the house."

"Sorry." Dee said with a huge grin on her face.

196

"What in the hell?" he said.

"I got arrested for hitting Kayla." Cheryl announced.

He didn't answer, instead he walked into his kitchen with Dee and Cheryl on his heels.

"You don't have anything to say?" Cheryl asked.

"What do you want me to say?"

"I don't know. Something more than nothing." she said with attitude.

"Well, since I couldn't say anything at your house, then I didn't think you would want me to say anything else."

"What is that supposed to mean?"

"Look you two, calm down…" Dee said stepping in between them.

"I guess you didn't tell Dee that you dismissed me earlier." he said while walking into the living room.

"I didn't dismiss you."

"No, you simply told me to call your disrespectful daughter for you, while your husband looked at me like I was the help!"

"I did no such thing. You are the one who got your ass on your shoulders and walked out the door!"

"No, you have it all wrong. When you need my help, it's oh Matthew, and please help me Matthew, but when you want to be all up in your ex-husbands ass, it's the opposite."

"How dare you!" Cheryl said while stepping closer to him.

"Now wait a minute." Dee held her hands up between them "Let's calm down. Cheryl, you didn't tell me that Matthew was with you earlier."

"Did that matter?"

"No, but why did you *dismiss* him, as he says."

"I didn't *dismiss* him. I asked him to leave so that we, me and Kevin, could talk to *our* daughter. Who knew he was so damn *sensitive*."

"I am not the *sensitive* one, maybe you need to talk to your gay son about that."

Cheryl's eyes got big and her mouth dropped open. She inhaled deeply and walked out of the kitchen.

"Cheryl, wait. I didn't mean that." he said to her back.

"You sure don't fight fair, do you?" Dee said to him while stepping outside.

"Dee, I didn't mean that. It...I...look, I'm trying to digest all that has happened today. Cheryl isn't the only one who got arrested today. I got picked up for defending my ex-wife against someone who was out to hurt her and Cheryl. It's a long story, but you have to tell Cheryl that I didn't mean it."

"You know Matthew. You are my boy, but sometimes y'all men are all alike, you stick your foot in your mouth and then you want someone else to clean up the mess."

"I'm not asking..."

"Why did you have to go and say the one thing that Cheryl's ex-husband always threw up in her face? Do you honestly believe that she doesn't know that Donnell is gay? Hell, she knew it before Donnell knew it. She always says that momma's know what their children will or will not be. She doesn't want him being singled out because of it, and she doesn't want him to feel unloved or unwanted as Kevin always made him feel. But for you to say that to her." She left the rest unsaid and walked away.

She got outside and Cheryl was standing by the car. She hit the remote to unlock the doors and Cheryl climbed inside. Dee shook her head as she walked to the other side of the car and got in.

As she pulled out of the driveway she asked if Cheryl wanted to go to dinner but she knew the answer would be no.

Dee tried to choose her words carely, "Cheryl..."

"Just take me home Dee." Cheryl said as she continued to stare out of the window.

Kayla bounced down the stairs after rushing her company out the side door and saw her dad in the kitchen. He was putting ice on his hand.

"What happened to your hand?"

"Nothing. Where were you? I called you when I got here almost ten minutes ago." he said while staring at his daughter standing in front of him with a short nightgown on. "Go put some damn clothes on".

"I was about to take a shower, I didn't hear you." she said.

She then noticed the scratches on his face and put her hand up to touch them when he slapped it away.

"What the fuck are you doing? Keep your fucking hands off of me." he yelled at her.

"Dang, who were you in a fight with? Did you go back over to mom's house and get into a fight with Matthew?"

"Don't you ever question me, do you hear me?" he said while slamming her against the counter.

"Daddy, stop!" she said as her eyes were as big as saucers.

He released her and cursed while walking out of the kitchen.

Chapter 41

Rebecca pulled herself up off of the floor, and limped into the kitchen. She dragged the ice cube tray from the freezer and put some in the dish cloth. She walked into the living room and pulled the cordless phone from the base.

"Can you come over? I need you." she whispered into the phone.

Her mother walked in and immediately started firing off the questions at Rebecca.

"What happened to you? Did Toni do this? You need to call the police, I told you she would be angry if you let her move down here with you and Kevin. You know those kind of people are jealous and violent."

"Mom, what people?" Rebecca said as she stepped away from her mother's embrace.

"You know. Gay people." She whispered.

"Mom, why are you whispering? No one can hear you."

"Well, I don't like to speak about such foolishness."

"Mom, please. I just want to lie down for a minute."

"Girl, you get your butt dressed. I'm taking you to the hospital."

"Mom, that is not necessary. I only have a few scratches and bruises. Nothing this ice won't fix." she said while sitting on the couch and folding her legs under her, while pressing the ice pack onto her lip.

"I don't know why you put up with…"

"Mom, don't. I will be fine. I just want you to sit with me. Please. Is that too much to ask?" she said while refusing to let the tears slip from her swollen eyes.

"You know your dad would be so upset if you are letting her start this again."

"I'm not. I promise." Rebecca said while getting up to get another towel, as her phone started to ring.

"My mom is here." she said and then was off of the phone.

"I know that wasn't that heifer." Her mother said.

"Heifer? Mom, who calls women that anymore?" she said with a smile.

"Well, I could call her much worse."

"That's why I love you." she said while snuggling up to her mother's ample breasts and resting her head like a two year old.

"I love you too." Her mother said as she brushed her daughter's wild hair down with her hands.

Rebecca's mother had only been gone for about thirty minutes when Toni appeared at her door. Rebecca immediately turned away from her.

As Toni stepped in front of her, "What the hell…"

"I know he didn't put his hands on you!" she shouted.

"Calm down, it ain't that serious." Rebecca said walking towards the kitchen.

"I know you are not about to tell me that you are letting him put his hands on you."

"Sit down!" Rebecca yelled back at her. "What's wrong, does it bring back memories?" she said as she placed her hands across her chest.

"I know you are not about…"

"Yeah I am. I am not going to stand here while you act all new. You used to do the same thing when we first met."

Toni stepped up to Rebecca, "that was a long time ago."

"Look, I don't feel like hearing it tonight."

"Did Kevin do this?"

"We had an argument, end of story."

"A story that normally ends with him beating a woman senseless."

"Look, if you're going to lecture me, go the hell on home."

"What? Is this about Atlanta?"

"I don't want to talk about it. What did you come over here for anyway?"

"I missed you, and since you ditched me at the mall, I wanted you to see what I bought today." she said while twirling around.

"Yeah, it looks good on you." Rebecca commented while maneuvering around her to go to the wet bar. "Do you want something to drink?"

"Yeah, dirty martini."

"Are you going to join me?" Toni asked walking up behind her. She spoke directly against her neck, in a sexy whisper, "I'm going to make you forget all about today."

Rebecca pushed against her, "And how do you propose to do that?"

"Well, for starters I would run you a nice hot bubble bath. You are a little tense, and from there, well, I'll let you decide."

Toni pinched Rebecca's nipples and whispered for them to go upstairs.

Toni ran Rebecca a hot bath and as Rebecca slid into the water her mind began to wonder about her situation. Tonight he proved that he was not going to change and the diamond ring on her finger only meant he wanted to control her, just like he did to Cheryl. Unlike Cheryl, Rebecca had that nigga by the balls. She just had to figure out what she planned on doing with all of her newfound information.

Chapter 42

Cheryl called Dr. Vorite's office and was told she had left for the evening. She called her cell phone and her cheerful voice answered immediately.

"Cheryl, I'm so glad you called. Is everything ok?"

"No." she said and immediately started crying.

"Ok, calm down. Where are you? Are you home?"

"Yes." she said between sobs.

"Give me your address, and I'll come over."

An hour later Cheryl opened the door and saw Dr. Vorite standing there.

"Would you like something to drink? I only have Pepsi and water, unless you want something stronger."

"Well, I'll take a Pepsi."

Cheryl went into the kitchen and opened a bottle of Pepsi and poured it into a glass.

She poured herself another glass of wine and joined the doctor in the living room.

"Um, do you think it wise for you to be drinking?"

"Why wouldn't it be?"

"Well, I don't want you to get in the habit of drinking whenever you feel stressed."

"Well, I don't normally drink." she said as she put the wine glass to her lips and drained half of it before placing it on the end table.

"Tell me what happened."

Cheryl explained all that happened between Kevin, Matthew, Kayla and herself.

"How did it make you feel when Matthew referred to your son as gay?"

"It hurt. He knew that Kevin always called my baby that. He knew that it upset me when Kevin did it, yet said it like it was nothing."

"Ok and what was your response?"

"What do you mean?"

"What did you say to him?"

"Nothing."

"Why not?"

"I don't know."

"Yes, you do. Why didn't you say anything?"

"I don't know." Cheryl said while getting up from the couch.

"Cheryl, yes you do know. Now tell me the truth, why didn't you say anything to him about calling your son gay?"

"Because..." her voice began to crack.

"Go on..."

"Because he is gay! My son is gay, but it doesn't matter to me." Cheryl said.

"Ok, so why didn't you tell Matthew that."

"I didn't want him to get mad."

"Get mad at who?" the doctor urged.

Cheryl shrugged her shoulders, trying not to say out loud what she was thinking.

"Who would he get mad with?"

"Me!" she blurted out. "He would get mad at me!"

"Why?"

"Because...because, I shouldn't question him."

"Question him about what?"

"I don't know. He doesn't like when I question him."

"Well, he said something about your child, why shouldn't you question him?"

"He'll just get mad and then, then…" her voice trailed off.

"Cheryl, are you ok?"

"I…I'm sorry. I was just thinking…"

"Tell me about it." the doctor looked into Cheryl's eyes.

"I…" her voice was barely above a whisper, "Kevin never liked when I questioned him about Donnell. That made it worst."

"And you think Matthew will do the same? You have to stop thinking every man is like Kevin. No one is like Kevin, except Kevin. You can't live your life scared to say what is on your mind."

Dr. Vorite touched Cheryl's hand.

"Ok, well, it's been a long day for you. I'll let you get some rest, and I will see you in a couple of days, for your regular appointment. Ok?"

"Ok, thank you for stopping by." she said, as she walked the doctor to the front door and held it open for her. As she walked past the answering machine, she saw the flashing number. She pressed the play button, heard the female's voice announcing the message and then she heard Matthew's voice.

Message one: Cheryl, please call me back, I'm sorry.

Delete

Message two: Cheryl, baby, please.

Delete

Message three: Girl, are you ok? You…

Delete

Message four: Mom, are you ok? Is Kayla behaving herself? I guess you went out tonight. Enjoy yourself, and I'll call later. I love you.

Message five: Cheryl, its Matthew again. I'm sorry, I should not have….

Delete.

Cheryl walked slowly to her room and sat in the chair and stared outside. She walked to the door leading to the private balcony off of her bedroom. The tears streamed down her face as her chest ached. It wasn't like a medical condition, it was more like her heart was breaking.

Chapter 43

Matthew wanted to call Cheryl one more time but decided against it when his phone rang.

"Cheryl?" he answered enthusiastically.

"No." said the cheerful voice. "Sherrie. I was feeling a little uneasy. Can you come over for a little while?"

"I'm tired. Can't it wait until tomorrow?"

"I...I just..."

"What's wrong?"

"I'm scared. Galen knows where I live and I don't want him coming here."

"Did he call?"

"No, but..."

"Ok, well, why don't you come over?" He hung up the phone and went to the closet and pulled on some jeans.

Cheryl picked up the phone on the third ring.

Dee asked her if she was ok.

"Yeah, I'm sleeping. What time is it?" Cheryl said as she rubbed her eyes and tried to focus on the clock.

"Oh, it's almost eleven."

"So you couldn't call me tomorrow?" she said while rolling her eyes.

"Well, I wanted to make sure you were ok. You know, with everything that happened today. I just wanted to make sure my girl was ok."

"I'm good."

"Really? Have you talked to Matthew?"

"No, he called."

Dee asked if he apologized.

"I didn't answer the phone."

"Look, don't punish him. He made a mistake, don't hold it against him."

"He called Donnell gay."

"I know, I was there. I think he was only mad, you know he wouldn't hurt you."

"But he did Dee. I don't know…"

"Are you serious? You let Kevin do far worse than that, and you forgave him over and over again. Matthew says something, granted he was totally out of line, but he has never done anything but love you, and you are ready to throw him back in the arms of his tramp of an ex-wife."

"I don't think…"

"Don't be naïve girl. That trick is up to something, and I don't trust her. She is a slick bitch and you better watch her. Did you hear what she said when we walked up to his crib today? She made a slick ass comment about why we were coming over to see *her* man. She thought I didn't hear her sneaky ass."

"Dee!"

"Sorry, I bet she is over there right now."

"I doubt it."

"How do you know? You are the one not taking his calls. If I only know one thing, I know how to comfort a man when his woman isn't."

"Why would he need comforting?"

"You don't know, do you? You weren't the only one getting locked up today. Matthew got locked up too, something to do with someone from his past."

"What! He didn't tell me that."

"Of course he didn't. You didn't give him a chance."

Cheryl was up from the bed, pulling on jogging pants and a shirt when she told Dee she needed to go.

"Where in the hell are you going this late?"

"To comfort *my* man."

"You better work it!" Dee yelled.

Matthew opened the door as he ex-wife slid past him.

"As you can see, I was ready for bed." He said to her as she walked past him.

"I won't stay long, I just needed to see you before I went to sleep."

"Well, have a seat. Are you ok? I mean, do you think you need to stay in a hotel for the night or something."

Sherrie told him she wasn't sure if she needed to be in a hotel.

"No matter what, you are the mother of my daughter and I don't want you to be hurt."

"Thank you Matthew." she said while sliding beside him on the couch and letting her head come to rest on his muscular chest.

"Matthew." she said breathlessly, while looking up at him.

"Sherrie." He said as he sucked in a quick breath.

She leaned more into him and kissed first his jaw, and then his cheek finally making her way to his mouth.

"Sherrie, we shouldn't…"

"Shh. Just let me…" she said as she continued to kiss him. She left his lips long enough to push his shirt up his chest. She felt his hands in her hair. She came back and looked at him. He thrust his tongue into her mouth while she let her left hand slid down further until she had a handful of his manhood.

The doorbell rang but Sherrie didn't stop instead she

continued to squeeze him.

"Sherrie...stop." he said while pushing her away from him. "I think you need to go."

"Matthew, you can't be serious." she said while sitting back on the couch."

He stood away from the couch as the doorbell sounded again.

"I am. This is a mistake and you and I both know it."

"Well, it doesn't *seem* like a mistake." she said while eyeing his crotch and the erection that was threatening to break through his jogging pants.

"Look, I need to get the door. I'll let you out." he said while pulling her up and towards the door.

He opened the door and before he could release Sherrie's hand, Cheryl fell into his arms and started kissing him.

"Matthew I'm sorry."

"Excuse me." Sherrie said and moved around them, bumping into Cheryl in the process.

"Sorry, didn't know anyone was here." Cheryl said as she wiped her mouth.

Sherrie responded by telling Matthew to call her later.

Matthew closed the door and pushed Cheryl against the foyer wall and pushed his tongue inside her mouth.

She started to speak but he shook his head no and continued to kiss her.

His hands roamed under her shirt and found her breasts free. His hand lifted the shirt above her head and he bent down and let his tongue slide across her erect nipples.

"Ahhh..."

"God, you are so beautiful." Matthew said as she lowered herself to her knees.

She pulled him free of his jogging pants and slid her mouth on him. His hands grabbed a fistful of her hair and he let out a loud groan.

He pushed her face into his groin faster and faster. She gagged a little and had to use her hands to stop him from pushing her too far. He pulled her up and turned her to face the wall. He guided himself into her and quickly pushed her to the point of orgasm. He felt her release herself onto him. He pulled away from her and led her to the couch where he took her again. Slapping skin was the only sound being made. No words, no moans, no grunts. Only skin against skin. He stopped suddenly and lifted her into his arms and carried her to his room.

He laid her down on his king sized bed. He climbed in beside her and she snuggled up to him. Their love making was fast at times, slow at others. Their moans and grunts filled his bedroom until they finished and Matthew collapsed on top of her before rolling off of her. He gathered her into his arms and they fell asleep.

Cheryl woke up first and had to adjust to the darkness in the room. As she moved his arm to get up from the bed. She heard him talking as she stood and she sat back down softly.

"Momma please...don't leave me. Momma, I love you, it's only me and you. You can't leave me in this world. Oh momma, please. Come back to me, please."

Cheryl shook him softly at first but when she noticed the tears roll from his closed eyes, she shook him awake.

His eyes opened slowly, "Cheryl?"

"Yes baby. What's wrong?"

"Nothing." he said as he got up and walked to the bathroom and shut the door.

Chapter 44

As Rebecca climbed out of the tub, Toni met her with a towel.

"Lie down and let me put some oil on you." Toni said while brushing her tongue against Rebecca's neck.

"...Toni."

"No, let me take care of you tonight."

Toni guided her over to her bed, and climbed onto the bed with her and straddled her back. She poured the vanilla oil from the bottle onto Rebecca's wet skin.

Rebecca moaned as Toni worked her hands down her body. She bent forward and let her teeth graze against the skin on Rebecca's back.

"Turn over for me." Toni said.

As she did, Toni used her tongue to start a trail of wet kisses down the front of Rebecca.

She pushed her tongued inside of Rebecca's mouth while her hands ran up and down her slim body.

Their lovemaking was becoming fast, furious and downright violent. They were hanging off of the bed as their orgasms rocked them both, threatening to throw them onto the floor.

Rebecca nudged Toni awake as she slid out of from under her. Her hair was unruly but she could see the discoloration of the marks on her neck, some because of Toni but the others were because of Kevin. She thought of how she would get Kevin to give her the Atlanta office. The things she uncovered about him and his mother was enough to ensure that the Atlanta office would no longer be up for discussion.

"Look Rebecca, I could lose my job if anyone found out I gave you *this* information."

"Look, it aint like you gave it to me for fucking free. I did pay your mortgage up and gave you five thousand to boot, so don't get all high and mighty now. I'm sure your wife would find it interesting that you like to play the high stakes game of poker, and never know when to quit, or win."

She said while snatching the envelope from Sam Baker "besides, when you were fucking my brains out you didn't seem to mind." She said with a twist of her lips.

He walked away from her and stood by the table, "I could lose my clearance for digging into somebody's background like this. I'm just saying, why you want to know about this Kevin Goldman guy anyway?"

"Let's just say, that I am doing my research for an upcoming project. Now why don't you come on over here so I can show you my appreciation?" she said, pulling him towards her.

She had no intention of having sex with him today so after five minutes of being on her knees, he was willing to give her all of the other information she needed.

Chapter 45

Cheryl rose from the bed and went downstairs to make herself a cup of tea before heading to her realtor's office. After last night, she knew Matthew had something in his past that he didn't want to share.

"Babe, do you want to talk about it?" she said when he came into the kitchen.

He opened up the refrigerator and asked her if she wanted something to drink.

"Matthew, I just asked you if you wanted to talk."

Instead of answering her, Matthew told her he would be back.

Cheryl walked back upstairs and sat in the sitting area of the bedroom. She curled her legs under herself and started drinking her tea.

He walked back into the room "You need to get some rest. It is only five in the morning."

"I'm ok. I need to get ready to see my realtor."

"I thought that meeting was at eight? "

"It is, I just thought you might want to talk."

"No, no reason to talk." He said as he sat beside her.

She rubbed her hand down his back, "look, I'm a great listener."

He turned and faced her, "Don't ok."

"What?" she said while still rubbing her hand up and down his back.

He turned away from her, "I don't want to talk about it."

"Sometimes it's better…"

He turned to her too quickly, causing her to lean away from him, "I'm sorry. Just don't push it. If I want to talk, I will but until then, don't ask me."

"Ok. Well I do have something else I want to ask." Cheryl said as he started to stand.

"What?" he sat back down.

"Why didn't you tell me that you were arrested yesterday?"

"You didn't seem to want to know." He said as his hard stare threatened to make her crumple.

"Baby, I always want to know when something happens to you. What happened?"

"Sherrie…"

"Never mind." She said as she rolled her eyes and sat her cup down.

Matthew chuckled as he rose and she stood with him. He kissed her on the forehead and walked out of the bedroom. She heard the double beep of the door and heard his car start.

As she pulled from the driveway her cellphone rang.

"Are you coming to get me today?" her daughter asked without saying hello.

"Umm, no. Remember you wanted to be with your dad, and until the court hearing on Monday, that is where you will be young lady."

"Tsk, I don't want to stay…"

"Too bad." Cheryl said as she hung up.

216

Chapter 46

Rebecca walked into Kevin's office and told him that they were set for the trip later that day to Atlanta.

Kevin put his arms around Rebecca's waist and tried to kiss her but she was all business.

"Look, I don't have time for this. I need to make sure that my... I mean the Atlanta office is running smoothly, so if you don't mind, get your head out of your pants and back on your shoulders." She said as she sidestepped him. "Besides after what happened a couple of days ago, you really don't want to go there with me." She said as she stood with her arms folded.

"Well, if you didn't get..."

"I know you are not about to say what I think."

"Well, I won't say it then." Kevin said as he walked away from her.

Rebecca made a comment about him not wanting to go until he found out that Toni was going.

Kevin spoke with attitude. "You never even told me that you were going. I don't give a flying fuck if Toni goes. You are acting like you are running this company..."

"No, corrections, I am running the Atlanta office, and whenever I feel I need to be there, is when I will be going there. Now, if you have a fucking problem with that..."

"Don't you for one second think that I won't take your fucking head off if you ever speak to me that way in my office."

Kevin said as he grabbed her.

Toni walked in. "Sorry to interrupt, but Joseph is on the phone."

As Rebecca snatched away from him, she gave him the look that let him know that this conversation wasn't over.

Chapter 47

Kevin rushed from his office and walked towards the reception area while Ashley went over the details with Rebecca for their upcoming trip.

"I'll meet you at the BWI, I forgot to make arrangements for Kayla. Ashley, also I will need you to go pick up my suit from the tailor, they said it's ready. I'll also need you to call Atlanta and let them know I will be there also, and will need use of the conference room. I think I'll show the T'wan around while down there. See if you can get him a flight out this afternoon, if not make sure he is on the earliest flight leaving tomorrow morning. Let's see if he knows how to act like a real star."

He pulled up in front of his house just as Kayla was coming in from school.

"Look, I'll be in Atlanta for the weekend but will be back on Monday before the hearing. You can stay here or do you want me to take you home?" Kevin said while walking upstairs and going into his closet to retrieve his suitcase and some suits. "I hope you can be trusted." he said as he continued pulling clothes from the closet and folded them into the open suitcase.

"Yeah, I'll stay here, I mean, what is there to do at home? At least I can hang out with some of my old friends."

"I'll be back in a couple of days. I'll leave you my ATM card in case you need something, only use it if you run out of cash."

he said as she followed him into the bathroom. She pulled his shaver, toothbrush, comb, brush and cologne from the cabinet and handed them to him.

They walked downstairs while he pulled his wallet and laid ten twenty dollar bills on the counter. He laid the ATM card on the counter and kissed her forehead and headed out the door.

Chapter 48

She arrived at her appointment earlier than expected. She couldn't believe that she was actually ready to see the therapist that Dr. Vorite suggested.

She began by telling the doctor what she had witnessed when she went by Matthew's office for lunch.

"...and he was all over her. I mean, he calls me there for lunch for me to catch him with his ex-wife. He could have told me that on the phone." She said as a tear slid down her face.

"Why are you so angry?" Dr. Cervantes asked.

"Because he had me believing that he actually loved me."

"So when you told him how you felt..."

Cheryl cut her off, "I didn't tell him, I just walked out."

"Why didn't you confront them?"

"What good would it have done? It wouldn't change the fact that he was practically having sex with her, right there in his office." Cheryl blew out a breath and closed her eyes to keep the remaining tears hostage.

"Cheryl, you need to stand up for yourself, for once. Do something for Cheryl, not because someone says it's ok, but because it *is* ok. When, and only when, you do that, you will see that you are the one who deserves to be loved unconditionally but it has to start with you. Like the Michael Jackson song says, start with 'the man in the mirror.'

Agony was not only on her face but in Cheryl's voice as she

spoke. "How do you start with the man in the mirror, when the man is scared to look in the mirror?"

"Why are you scared to look in the mirror?"

After a long pause, Cheryl answered "...because I don't know what I am going to see."

"What do you think you are going to see?"

"I don't...

"Well, why not start right now?"

"I really don't think..."

Dr. Cervantes pulled her from the seat and guided her towards the mirror that she kept on the wall beside the bathroom. She stood behind Cheryl as she struggled to lift her eyes to look in the mirror.

"You need to look at yourself Cheryl. I mean, really look at yourself."

A tear formed in the corner of Cheryl's eye and she looked away.

Dr. Cervantes allowed her to walk away from the mirror as she spoke, "Cheryl, you need to re-adjust your self-image. Only you can do that. You have to stop letting your son, your ex-husband, the new man in your life, and now your daughter, define your self-image. You let your husband take away your identity. You became his wife, then a mother, then a soccer mom, a part-time valet and yet he didn't allow you to be the one thing you wanted to be, his partner in and out of the bedroom. You let your son become your friend, instead of being his mother. You let this new man become your rescuer, you are letting him fight your battles for you, you are looking for him to be your answer when you don't have one, you are looking for him to solve your problems and now you are letting Kayla take the place of Kevin. You are handing control over to her, she tells you what she will and will not do, and now she is hitting you. Yes, I can still see the bruise. I am sure you were going to try and explain it away as something else, but I kind of figured when you called and said it had something to do with Kayla that the bruise on the side of your face wasn't because you ran into a cabinet or something."

"You don't understand what it's like."

"Then tell me."

"My entire life I have felt unloved, and Kevin comes along. He was a knight in shining armor, he swept me off my feet, but quickly dropped me soon after we got married. However, I never thought about leaving him, I never considered leaving him because that is not what I was taught."

The doctor looked over her glasses, "What were you taught?"

Cheryl got up and started pacing around the doctor's office like a caged lion at the circus, "I was taught that you stay with your man, no matter what. You don't leave a marriage when you get tired of it. The only way you leave is if you catch your husband in adultery."

"Didn't you catch him with another woman?"

"Well, not at first…"

Dr. Cervantes pressed harder, "and when you did…"

"When I did, I begged him to stay." Cheryl let out a nervous laugh. "He even asked me for a divorce when he was out of town on a, quote unquote, business meeting. Called me from his hotel room and said it like he was asking for a cheeseburger in the drive thru, and I begged him like a crack addict begging a dealer for a hit. I even caught him in his office, riding that tramp like a damn dog. I still didn't leave him. It wasn't until Donnell graduated that I left, and only then, I did it because Kevin had went out and bought a townhouse and announced that he had asked Rebecca to marry him. Then I left, but do you want to know why? I left because I was embarrassed. Can you believe that? I was embarrassed and to save face, I left. How sick is that?"

Cheryl laughed and then broke down into a hysterical cry. A cry that racked her entire body. She fell to her knees and Dr. Cervantes rushed to her and wrapped her arms around the crying woman.

Cheryl was able to compose herself enough to get to the chair.

"Cheryl, let me ask you a question. You seem as if you have been holding that in for a very long time. You really need to slow down, you seem to be overwhelmed and that is not good. You are losing weight. I have noticed a little hair loss and you are packing on the makeup in the morning. I am not trying to make you feel bad, but you are wearing yourself out. I think you should think about going into treatment…"

"No, I can't do that. Kevin…"

"This is not about Kevin, this is about you and your mental state."

"I can't go into a hospital for crazy people. I just can't…"

"Well, I could prescribe something for you, something that will take the edge off. Let me ask you, are you sleeping very well?

She shook her head no and the doctor went to her desk, wrote out a prescription and handed it to her. Cheryl walked out of her office feeling exhausted. She sat in her truck and closed her eyes.

She looked at her phone when it vibrated and noticed several missed calls and that she had four messages.

Cheryl, this is Matthew, I am sorry I missed you. I tried calling but I guess you are tied up. Call me as soon as you get this message.

The next message was from Kevin telling her that he was going out of town and to check on Kayla, since she was home alone.

This is Matthew again. I was hoping you were coming by. Call me as soon as you can. I love you baby.

224

She gave a half laugh. "Really, you love me. Well I couldn't tell this afternoon." She said out loud to no one.

The next message was from Dee but she deleted it since she had no intention of going anywhere but to bed. But before that could happen she had to check on Kayla.

She walked in to find girls half naked sprawled across men old enough to be their father. She smelled the marijuana and alcohol as she made her way to the kitchen. Not finding her daughter, she climbed the stairs and opened the door to her daughter's room. The man was standing at the bed and her daughter was bent over it. Cheryl wasn't sure what she screamed but the man looked at her with a smile and wink. Cheryl went to the bed, yanked Kayla upwards and told the man that her daughter was 15 and that she was calling the police. His smile quickly left him and he bolted from the room while Kayla sulked on the bed.

Cheryl ran down the stairs but the house was clearing out as if the SWAT team was on its way. She pulled her phone out and made one more call.

"Look, I need to get back to Maryland, there is an emergency with Kayla."

Rebecca only half listened.

"Ok, well, I have the meeting in the morning with Mr. Mickey and Steven will also be there. Is there anything that you want me to bring up?"

"Uh, no, but there is something we need to discuss before I leave."

Rebecca's face showed annoyance, "ok, what is it?"

"The running of this office."

"Ok. I think it is going just fine." She said with a grin.

"I'm glad you think so. However, I will start to interview

225

people next week."

"For what?"

"As office manager. I will need you more in the Maryland office. I hired Toni to help you out, so now you can spend more time on our clients there."

"You hired Toni because *you* needed an office manager."

"Yes, and now that we have acquired Alpine Hotels and Spas, I need both of you to work on that, not running…"

Rebecca came from behind her desk, "I will not give up the Atlanta office. You promised."

"And here we go again. I didn't give you anything…"

"Oh, but you will." she said as she walked over to the file cabinet.

"What did you say to me?" Kevin said as he grabbed her arm.

"Get your hands off of me! I didn't stutter, I said you will give this to office to me." She opened up the drawer and took out the manila envelope. "I suggest you look at these before you go." She said while handing him the envelope.

Kevin threw the envelope back at her. "I don't need to look at shit! This is my company, not yours."

"I don't want your fucking company. I want this office and I want 5%."

"5% of what?"

"Stocks. I did my research. Your company is growing at a faster rate, than even you and Corey ever realized. You and Corey started with a 50/50 split. All I'm asking is that I get some of that."

"You are fucking crazy!"

"Like a fox. The way I see it, you don't have a choice." she walked over and picked up the folder, stretching it out before him. "Before you say no, I suggest you open up that envelope and do a little reading, then give me your answer when I get back to Maryland."

"I don't take too kindly to threats." Kevin said while his jaw clenched.

"It's not a threat my dear, its insurance. When I first started you always told me to keep my eyes and ears open, because you never knew when an opportunity would present itself. I only did as I was told, and now my opportunity has come. Now, happy reading, I have a meeting to get to and you have a flight to catch."

Kevin arrived back in Maryland and was fuming by the time he reached Cheryl's house. Cheryl had barely opened the door when he pushed by her and was yelling for Kayla.

"Tell me what emergency you had with Kayla that made me rush all the way back here." He said as he walked into the living room.

"Your daughter was caught with a man old enough to be you and there was drinking and smoking."

Her words were cut off by Kevin yelling for Kayla.

"She's in the kitchen." Cheryl said.

Kevin brushed by her on the way to the kitchen, where Kayla was sitting at the table.

"You have ten fucking seconds to start talking or so help me, you will need to dial 911 right now!" Kevin said while slamming his hand down on the counter.

Cheryl moved in front of her daughter, "Look, stop screaming and let her talk."

Kevin shouted and took one step towards the table, "Shut the fuck up! I wasn't talking to you!"

"But..." Kevin took another step and Cheryl stopped talking. He walked over to Kayla and snatched her up from the chair. He raised his hand,

"Kevin, don't!" Cheryl said while grabbing his arm.

"Get off of me!" Kayla said while snatching away from him.

227

"Don't you ever…" he yelled before slapping Kayla so hard that the pins holding her hair on top of her head, flew across the kitchen. Cheryl ran over to pull him away from Kayla. "Who in the fuck do you think you are? I didn't leave you in my house to throw a fucking party!"

"Get your hands off of me!" Kayla yelled while trying to pull from his grasp.

Cheryl did her best to stop the ruckus from getting totally out of hand. "Kevin wait a minute! Let's calm down…"

He turned towards her. His chest heaved and he gulped in air.

"Calm down! Are you fucking kidding me? You called me to tell me that my fifteen year old daughter has an emergency and I come home and you tell me that there was underage drinking going on. Do you know what could happen if the police had run up in there? Do you?

"I'm calling the police!" Kayla yelled while holding her hand to her face. She pulled her cellphone from her pocket.

"Kayla sit down!" Cheryl walked quickly towards her daughter and took the phone from her hand.

"…are you serious, I'm not you, I'm not letting him hit on me!" Kayla shouted at her mother.

"What the fuck does that mean!" Kevin said advancing towards his daughter again.

"It means, that you beat mom all the time and she never called the police. Well I am not her."

Kevin's face contorted in anger, "How dare you say that to me!"

"It's the truth!" Kayla shouted back.

"What have you been telling this girl?" Kevin said as he walked towards Cheryl.

"How dare you! She has seen you." Cheryl yelled.

Kevin now beside Cheryl, "You better close your mouth."

"No! I'm so sick of it, always trying to run shit over here.

God only knows I put up with it while we were married but this is my house!"

"Only because I pay for it!"

"You are only paying for it because you don't want the truth to come out!"

"What truth would that be?"

"That you are a wife beater and..." something stopped her from continuing.

"And what?"

"Nothing," she said and tried to move away. Kevin stood firmly in front of her. "I think you should go."

As she tried to move around him, he pushed her.

"Answer me, and what Cheryl?"

"Nothing, just leave." she said as she managed to get away from him.

"Answer my fucking question, what were you going to call me?" he challenged as he walked behind her. When she reached for the door, he grabbed her arm.

"Get off of me Kevin!" she yelled trying to free herself from his grasp.

"You better tell me or so help me..." he squeezed her arms tighter.

"Stop it, you're hurting me!"

"Tell me!"

"A rapist, you are a rapist!"

Before she could brace herself, he had slapped her so hard it knocked her into the door and then the floor.

"Don't you ever call me that!" Kevin said, while spit flew from his mouth.

"You are," she said while holding the side of her face and scooted away from him. He grabbed her by the shirt and picked her up, he back-handed her and sent her falling to the floor again.

Cheryl continued, "You raped me while we were married and

not more than a month ago. You can't stand that somebody might want me. You are a hateful man, an evil, hateful man. For years, you made me feel less of a woman, made me feel like I didn't matter, but you know what, I do matter, not because you say so, but because I say so. You have some issues, something that you need to get counseling for, maybe something happened to you in your childhood that…"

"Don't ever bring up my childhood." He said as he slapped her again, drawing blood from her mouth.

She sucked her bottom lip and steadied herself against the wall. She continued to speak, "You hide behind your business. You think that everyone owes you something. No one owes you a damn thing. You are sick Kevin, and you need help."

"No, what I need is for you to stop nagging me all the fucking time!"

"And what I need, is for you to get out of my house." she said after she pulled herself up from the floor. She walked into the kitchen to get a cloth for her bleeding mouth. She knew the decision she was about to make would change her life forever.

Chapter 49

Kevin got home and poured himself a drink. He glanced down at the manila envelope on the desk. He opened it and found the letter from Rebecca.

Kevin, I didn't want to have to do this, but you leave me no choice. Enclosed in this envelope are computer printouts of conversations you have been having with 'kissmehard.'

I'm sure your mouth is hanging open, and if I know you as I think I do, you are most likely having a stiff drink right now, go ahead take a sip, because you are going to need it.

First, I tried to be reasonable with you, but you weren't doing the same with me. I asked you nicely about the Atlanta office and you laughed in my face. Well, guess who is laughing now. I am, because you see, kissmehard is my good friend, Stanley, and he is as gay as your son. If you don't believe me, look at the pictures that I have taken. See, the one with him on the computer about a month ago, I took it on my cell, notice the time stamp, I highlighted so you could see it clearly, and turn the picture over, you will see your entire conversation. I think you got a little upset when he wanted to do anal, tsk, tsk, tsk. What a shame, sometimes Stanley gets a little carried away, but he always called and told me how nice and horny he would leave you.

Secondly, look at the last ten pages, does that look familiar to you? I am not unsympathetic to you, I know it must have been hard to bury your mother at such an early age. I am sure that your mother couldn't stand the fact that the man in her life was doing all of those perverted things to you. Your poor mother must have been scared to death when she found out that her son, had been raped by her man, or did she get mad because you had him and she didn't. You see, Calvin, I think you remember him, and my friend, Stanley, well they are partners now and he started telling Stanley all about this crazy ass man, named Henry, who would beat up his girlfriend and then offer her to the highest bidder, and how old Henry would be fucking her son. I'll give you one guess on her son's name. I guess you didn't hide your skeletons too well.

It's a damn shame that I had to resort to this, but you left me no choice. Now, as I have been asking, I want the Atlanta office. I am even willing to forego the 5% in the company, if and this is a big if, you give me Atlanta, that means, you get no income from it, and neither does Corey. Ok, since it was your money that built it, you can come down to see how it is running, you can even give input if you would like. For the first three years, it will stay under the K & B Alliance umbrella, however, after that it will become my company. I will pay you a handsome fee of at least one million dollars, but no more than five, regardless of how much money it makes, because I know this office will be as successful as the one in New York and the one in DC.

Now if you choose not to accept this offer, I will be forced to send these emails, pictures and instant messages to the magazines and your inner circle of contacts and you do know what they love to do to us black folks, when we fall from grace. Never mind the fact that they might not want to do business with a man that has been a wife beater.

Now, I will be back in Maryland sometime Tuesday morning. I expect my answer then. Remember you always told me, always keep your eyes and ears open, you never know what you might hear.

Love you always,
Rebecca Hardy

PS. I will keep the ring as a parting gift.

Kevin threw his glass against the wall in the den. He grabbed the phone.

"You have a fucking nerve trying to blackmail me!"

"I see you finally opened up the envelope and it's not blackmail sweetie, its facts, which you didn't hide too well. Now, I don't expect an answer today..."

"You aren't getting shit from..."

"Now, now, why must you use such language? I *will* get the office and here is why, besides that envelope, oh and those are not the originals, remember when you got a little grabby a little while back, well I did file a report, but I have a friend that is holding on to it. Now, your little weak ass ex-wife didn't press charges against your ass, but I will. Good bye and see you Tuesday."

He hung up just as the doorbell rang.

"Mr. Kevin Goldman?"

"Yes."

"Can you step outside please?"

"What seems to be the problem?" he said as he stepped out and saw there were two more police cars pulling up in front of the house.

"Turn around and place your hands behind your back."

"What the hell is going on?"

"Sir, place your hands..."

"Not until you tell me what the hell is going on."

"I'm not going to ask you again." The police officer said

233

while he placed his hand on his holster.

Kevin turned around and the officer quickly put the handcuffs on him and led him to his car.

"Can I at least know what I am being arrested for?"

"Well, you are being arrested for domestic violence against your ex-wife and your daughter this evening."

"Are you serious?"

"Yes sir. Now please watch your head as you get in."

Chapter 50

Galen's patience had paid off. Cheryl was a creature of habit, going to her doctor every Tuesday and Thursday, although today she had to stop at the Walgreen's, but other than that, her day was just like all the rest. Her bratty daughter wasn't home, but she would get there soon enough and that would be an extra bonus.

As he climbed the two stairs, he took out the bump key and used it to open the door effortlessly.

Donnell

"Are you sure you want to do this?"

Donnell gave him a look, "Yeah, that bitch doesn't know who she is fucking with. She thinks she is so damn smart, but I'll get the last laugh."

"Do you think your dad will believe you?"

"I don't care if he does, she won't be able to hide the fact that her best friend is also her lover."

Donnell and his lover sat on the couch and watched as the DVD played. Rebecca and her lover Toni were naked on the bed in the bedroom.

Donnell stopped the video and pushed the note and DVD into the waiting envelope, that was already addressed to Kevin and Rebecca. The messenger arrived just as he finished putting the tape on the second envelope. He handed them both to the young woman and shut the door with a huge smile on his face.

Rebecca

"Toni, are you ready to move to Atlanta?"

"As long as you and I are together, I don't care where we move to." Rebecca pulled Toni closer and kissed her.

Her doorbell rang and the young woman handed her the envelope. Rebecca closed the door and shook the envelope.

"Who is it from?" Toni asked.

"Has to be from Kevin. Sounds like our future is in this envelope." She said as she began to tear open the package.

B. Swangin Webster

Cheryl and Mathew

Matthew tried calling her once more but when she didn't answer again, he knew what he had to do. It had been two days since he heard from her and he was beginning to get worried. He finished up at the office and he arrived at his house and told Lynette that he would be back. Hopefully with Cheryl by his side, but at this point he couldn't be so sure.

He drove to her house and there were no lights on, but her car was in the driveway. He wasn't leaving until he saw her. He secretly hoped that she hadn't seen Sherrie all over him but he knew this had to be the only reason she was not returning his calls.

He got out of the car and walked up to the door. As he pressed the doorbell, he felt the box in his pocket. He said a prayer as she opened the door.

"Matthew." She started to say when a hand yanked her away from the door.

Before Matthew could say anything Galen had a gun to Cheryl's head and motioned with the gun for Matthew to come inside.

"You really are as stupid as I thought you were." Matthew said as he crossed the threshold and saw the overturned foyer table and a small amount of blood oozing from Cheryl's nose.

Her mouth was swollen but he could see the swelling under her right eye as well.

"You should have killed me when you had the chance."

"Oh, I will." Matthew said as he walked towards him while Galen held firmly to Cheryl. "So, how do you want this to end? Quick and easy or slow and painful?"

Matthew was unbuttoning his shirt as he saw the beads of sweat appear across the lip of Galen. He also saw the unmistakable signs of someone in need of a hit of something.

"You see, someone like you can't go too long without their drug. Now what is yours? Crack, Meth? It has to be one or the other. What you didn't count on was that she would put up a fight, did you? I taught her well." Matthew turned his attention to Cheryl.

"Baby are you ok?" he said as he touched her face and felt the swelling under her eye.

She was trembling but nodded yes as the lone tear slid down her face. It was then that he noticed her blouse was ripped and she didn't have on pants.

He felt a tear forming in his eye and his breath became rapid. His jaw clenched and he knew that he needed to be quick or it could cost her life.

"The fight has taken more out of you than you expected. So, either you let her go right now or I promise you, I will make you suffer. Your choice." He said as he continued to advance toward them. They had come to rest in the living room and Matthew kept looking to his left.

"No, you under-estimated me. You thought you were so smart. But I had your wife."

"Correction, ex-wife." Matthew said.

"Whatever, I had her nine ways to Sunday and this one here...well let's just say she got a little taste of what I could do."

He lowered the gun to her thigh and Matthew heard her

inward gasp as another tear fell from her eye.

That was the moment that Matthew needed. As Galen looked away for a split second, Matthew lowered his shoulder and tackled Cheryl and Galen. His arms were wrapped around Cheryl as to break her fall but Galen hit the floor hard. Cheryl rolled away and scrambled towards the kitchen. Matthew scampered on his hands and knees over to Galen as he scrambled to recover the dropped gun. Galen had the gun in his hand and swung and connected with the side of Matthew's face. Blood poured from the open wound just above Matthew's temple. Matthew punched at the air as the blood stung his eye but connected at the knee of Galen, sending him crashing down to the floor.

Matthew was able to get to his feet and pulled Galen up with him. He gathered Galen by the shirt and punched him twice in the stomach, stealing his breath and then hit him with a left punch that sent Galen sailing over the couch. Galen groaned from behind the couch as Matthew stood over him. Galen didn't move until Matthew got close enough and then Galen swept Matthew's feet from under him, sending him crashing down beside him. Galen got up and kicked Matthew in the stomach but as the second kick came towards him, Matthew grabbed his ankle and twisted. The cracking sound was not as loud as the howl from Galen as his ankle exploded through the skin. Galen fell, yelling in pain as Matthew looked around for the gun.

Galen's eye bulged as he saw the gun being aimed at him.

Matthew turned to see Cheryl holding the gun.

"Baby, it's ok, give me the gun."

Her stare was hard as she shook her head no.

"Cheryl, baby, give me the gun." Matthew said as he saw her hand begin to shake.

"That bitch don't have it in her." Galen said from the floor.

"No, no. Not again. I am not weak. I'm not." Cheryl said as she smiled and blew out a breath. "You are just like him and unless I stop you, you will do it again."

Matthew moved closer to Cheryl. "Baby, give me the gun. You don't want to do this."

Her voice was shaky but calm. "But I do. I can't let him do this to anyone else."

"You are not going to shoot me because you are just like his momma." He said motioning his head towards Matthew. "That dumb bitch..." before he got the rest of the words out, Matthew had kicked him in the stomach.

"Don't you ever say anything about my mother!" Matthew shouted as he kicked him twice.

"I'm not weak." He heard Cheryl say from behind him. "I'm not weak, not anymore." The tears were streaming down her face as Matthew rose and walked towards her.

"No!" she shouted as Matthew stopped and held his hands up. "Move!'

Matthew took a couple of steps to the side. "Baby, just give me the gun..."

Before he could get the rest of the sentence out, she had fired. The first shot hit Galen in the left leg but the second one hit him in the chest. Matthew walked slowly to Cheryl and when he reached her, she collapsed into his arms and he let his tears join hers.

The coroner, the police and the detectives stayed and questioned Cheryl and Matthew separately for hours.

He could hear her sobs from the other room and he couldn't take it. He had long finished but she was still being questioned. She finally emerged. Her curly hair was unruly, her eyes were bloodshot red and her right eye was almost closed. The blood around her nose had dried and she had a split lip.

Her head was lowered as he whispered her name and she raised her eyes to meet his.

"I'm ok." She said to Matthew.

"I know baby."

"I love you." she said.

"I love you too." He said as he pulled her into his arms. "Nothing will change that and nothing or no one will ever hurt you again."

THE END

Let Me Say This, Again

B. Swangin Webster

Biography

B. Swangin Webster is an accomplished novelist with two novels to her credit. She is also a talk show host on WLVS Radio; streaming live on computers in 21 countries and the USA. Her talk show, The We B Swangin Show focuses on the latest in the publishing industry, authors and her love of shoes.

B. Swangin Webster attributes her success to consistently being in front of people and loving what she does.

When she is not writing or thinking of her next novel; she enjoys spending time in the kitchen and playing with her nine grandchildren.

CPSIA information can be obtained at www.ICGtesting.com
Printed in the USA
BVOW04s1243080415

395289BV00002B/7/P